THE LEGACY SERIES

SERIES TITLES

Like Human
Janet Goldberg

The Hopefuls
Elizabeth Oness

Never Stop Exiting
Michael Hopkins

Broken Heart Syndrome
Anne Colwell

The Mexican Messiah: A Novella & Stories
Jay Kauffmann

Close to a Flame
Colleen Alles

American Animism
Jamey Gallagher

Keeping What's Best Left Kept Secret
David Ricchiute

Soaked
Toby LeBlanc

The Path of Totality
Marie Zhuikov

Shocker in Gloomtown
Dan Libman

The Continental Divide
Bob Johnson

The Three Devils and Other Stories
William Luvaas

The Correct Response
Manfred Gabriel

Welcome Back to the World: A Novella & Stories
Rob Davidson

Greyhound Cowboy and Other Stories
Ken Post

Taken together, the thirteen stories of John Loonam's *The Price of Their Toys* slowly and artfully unravels the security blanket our fathers and grandfathers once tried, so clumsily, to wrap around our shoulders. It is the same blanket they tried to wrap themselves in when they left their wars and their cities and their terrors behind for the safety and forgetfulness of the suburbs. The world they built for us was never safe and nothing was forgotten. *Toys* is a vivid, powerful coming-of-age tale, a story of stories. There is deep longing but there is also perseverance and resilience, hope of repair and glimmering humor. It is all illuminated by the dim street lamps, the boozy neon signs, and the faint yellow headlights of Long Island. Each story is beautifully set and rendered. These are our young men and boys, dear reader. They are trying to find their way without a compass.

—FRANK HABERLE
author of *Downlanders*

THE PRICE OF THEIR TOYS

STORIES OF MEN AND BOYS

John P. Loonam

CORNERSTONE PRESS
UNIVERSITY OF WISCONSIN-STEVENS POINT

Cornerstone Press, Stevens Point, Wisconsin 54481
Copyright © 2026 John P. Loonam
www.uwsp.edu/cornerstone

Printed in the United States of America.

Library of Congress Control Number: 2026930400
ISBN: 978-1-968148-34-8

Cornerstone Press titles are produced in courses and internships offered by the Department of English at the University of Wisconsin–Stevens Point.

DIRECTOR & PUBLISHER
Dr. Ross K. Tangedal

EXECUTIVE EDITORS
Jeff Snowbarger, Freesia McKee

EDITORIAL DIRECTOR
Brett Hill

SENIOR EDITORS
Paige Biever, Ellie Atkinson

PRESS STAFF
Samantha Bjork, Sophie McPherson, Madison Schultz, Autumn Vine, Lillian Kulbeck, Karlie Harpold, Eleanor Belcher, John Evans, Christiana Niedzwiecki, Lilli Resop, Grady Roesken, Andrew Bryant

for
ELEEN HERBERT JORDAN
il miglior fabbro

ALSO BY JOHN P. LOONAM:

Music the World Makes

STORIES

The difference between men and boys is the price of their toys.

—Doris Rowland

Running

Shortly after his mother drove the family station wagon into the lobby of the RKO Twin on Sunrise Highway, Martin Harrigan walked to Sam Pearlstein's house for the first time. In the weeks since the Pearlsteins had moved from Kew Gardens and their chubby, curly-haired son had befriended him, Martin had simply stood in his own backyard, which adjoined the one that now belonged to the Pearlsteins, and waited for Sam to come out. That had worked well enough, but now Martin's mother, Bunny Harrigan, needed time to fill out insurance forms and sent Martin out to circle the block and approach from the sidewalk.

On the way, Martin kept his hands in the pockets of his corduroy jacket, noticing that despite the May chill Mrs. Hennessey's garden had flowers blooming in neat rows, the Santos' lawn was cut and fertilized, and Mr. Madorsky was trimming the hedge that separated his front yard from the Friedman's. When he got to the Pearlsteins', he stood on the sidewalk a full minute studying how even the hedges were with the bottom of the windows, trying to decide whether to go to the formal front door, or slip up the driveway to the friendlier kitchen door on the side of the house, all the time wishing he could just wait in his own backyard with its toys and sports equipment hidden in the tall grass, and hope that sooner or later Sam would come out and find him.

Bunny had not been going fast, she explained to the officer. She had, in fact, been stopped at the red light on Morris Avenue lighting a cigarette before taking her foot off the brake to retrieve the lighter she had dropped on the floor over on the passenger side.

"I couldn't let the car burst into flames," she said. The officer scribbled in his notepad as Bunny gently nudged the cigarette lighter, which she had carried out of the car, into his line of vision. Martin watched the officer not looking up at his mother. "If you look close," she said, "there's a burn mark on the mat, so I was doing the right thing." By then, Martin, Elaine and Milton were on the sidewalk, several yards away from the car which was still jutting into the lobby of the RKO, having pushed in the plate glass doors.

The theater manager, a teenager Martin was certain would have a sister in his grade, walked the length of the station wagon, crunching broken glass under his black shoes, waving his arms and pointing at the hanging shards of aluminum and the crack in the glass panel of the ticket booth. He described each detail he pointed at, "You've destroyed the front door. There's broken glass everywhere." His maroon manager's jacket was too small and hunched up nearly to his elbows, exposing a tan line at his wrists. Finished with the outside damage, he crunched back across the sidewalk and pushed the hanging aluminum aside to examine the lobby. "This carpet is going to have to be replaced. There are tire treads on it."

"Thank God no one was hurt," Mrs. Harrigan spoke again to the officer, who still did not look up from his pad. "This really could have been much worse." She gestured toward the candy counter, a dozen feet across the lobby where Mrs. Leviton, the silver-haired woman who worked afternoons selling popcorn and Twizzlers and who looked to Martin like she probably knew his piano teacher, stood with her arms folded sternly across her chest.

The officer continued writing.

The car had not been going very fast. It had simply drifted under the power of the drivetrain across four lanes of traffic, up the curb onto the sidewalk to push against the glass doors, which might have survived had not Bunny, in her panic, mistaken the gas for the brake and given it just enough extra push to shatter the entranceway and thrust the engine and the front seat into the lobby, leaving the back seat and the long trunk outside, blocking the sidewalk. Now the car could not be moved until the fire department came, though neither the manager nor Mrs. Harrigan could understand why, the repeated phrase "There's no fire," being the only thing they could agree on, with Bunny Harrigan waving the cigarette lighter in the officer's face for emphasis.

Milton, Martin's younger brother, pointed to the poster for *The Jungle Book* that hung lopsided by a single staple attaching its upper left corner to what remained of the "Coming Soon" frame beside the ticket booth.

"Can we go? Saturday?" he asked.

Elaine, Martin's older sister, poked Milton in the head with all four stiffened fingers.

"Shut up, jerk face."

Martin went to wait in the back seat of the car.

"I'm on the clock here, Bunny," Tom Harrigan, Martin's father, said as he paced the floor, one hand pulling at his hair, the other waving his cigarette in front of his chest as if conducting an orchestra only he could hear.

"There's quite a lot of paperwork," Bunny said, showing him the pile of insurance forms the theatre manager had given her. "I could use a little help. Legal advice." She touched her husband's arm gently, then held on when he tried to move away.

"I have the McDermott closing and the Silver contract…" Tom waved the cigarette in time to the silent symphony.

Ashes dusted his bare feet. Mr. Harrigan had a law office in Manhattan, but had, for all intents and purposes, stopped going in. He announced every morning at breakfast that commuting was a waste of time, that he had too much work to bother with trains and buses, that the country air would do him good. He kept a card table and a typewriter in the attic. He wore a plain dark suit and brightly colored bowtie every day, but had stopped putting on shoes and socks. He had been working on the McDermott closing and the Silver contract for months, though sometimes it was the McDermott contract and the Silver closing.

The station wagon sat in the driveway, broken glass and scratched paint visible on the hood of the car. Bunny narrated the incident from the long grass of the front lawn, imitating Elaine's short shriek as the car narrowly missed a Volkswagen while crossing Sunrise Highway and including sound effects for the crack and tinkle of the broken glass that hit the sidewalk as well as the deeper drumbeat of the shards that bounced off the hood of the car. Her voice was loud and dramatic in her attempt to reach Tom, who stared out the window at her, furtively parting the curtain with one hand while conducting the silent symphony with the other. When Bunny tried to get him to come outside and assess the damage, he mumbled "McDermott," and retreated up the stairs, his bare feet slapping at each step.

When Bunny got back to the kitchen, the children had retreated to the TV room, where the set was too loud. Bunny sat on a stool at the counter and studied the insurance papers. They were full of blank lines where she was to fill in information, blocks of small print she would have to read, and several large empty squares in which she was to draw a diagram of the accident, labeling the traffic rule indicators according to a legend printed in the margin. She had not drawn anything since art school and closed her eyes now to try to envision the intersection of Morris Avenue and Sunrise Highway, the glass doors of the RKO Twin, and the length of the station wagon, as seen from the roof. She smiled and arranged the papers in a line along the kitchen counter so she could easily move from one page to the next. She went to the old Chock Full o' Nuts coffee can full of pens and pencils beside the phone and—after rejecting a ball-point pen from Starburst Dry Cleaners and a crayon Milton had left there—found two pencils with nice sharp points. When she returned to the line of papers at the counter, she discovered page 3 was lying in a circle of spilled milk and a dark wet spot had seeped through the first of the boxes she was to draw in.

Bunny sucked in a deep breath through pursed lips, like whistling in reverse and began clapping her hands, slowly and loudly, calling the name of a child with each clap.

"Elaine." Clap

"Martin." Clap.

"Milton." Clap.

"Elaine." Clap.

"Martin."

None of the children actually entered the kitchen; Elaine and Milton bunched in the doorway; Martin peeked around the frame.

Bunny Harrigan opened her mouth and took a deep breath with which to yell at her children. But she caught herself, smiled tightly and—her voice high as she spoke rapidly—said, "Too much television! Everybody out!" She began to clap again—faster this time, more like applause. "Fresh air. You spent all morning in the car, now you are cooped up in the house? Out! Out!"

Elaine began to argue but Bunny cut her off, "Elaine, be a good big sister and take Milton to the playground. Martin, go visit that nice new boy from Queens."

Martin knew not to argue when his mother was talking fast. He took his brown corduroy jacket off the hook by the door. "What time should we be home?"

Bunny's voice strained brightly with false enthusiasm. "Call if you decide to eat dinner at your friend's house. We're having sandwiches!"

Martin knew even before Mrs. Pearlstein appeared at the kitchen door and invited him in that her kitchen would smell different than his own. Every kid's house smelled different. They all knew it, but collectively pretended they could not distinguish the wine, cigarettes and sour milk of his own house from the Vitrovs' sweat and bacon, the Santinos' garlic and Pine Sol or the Fishmans' overloaded electrical circuits, so Martin was pleasantly surprised by the chicken soup and paint thinner of the Pearlsteins'. He inhaled carefully and decided that the smell was gentle and inviting.

Mrs. Pearlstein was excited to see him, reacting as if they were old friends. She offered to take his jacket, bending over so that her round face smiled directly into his, though she was only a few inches taller than he to begin with. She reached out as if to help him remove the coat but stopped just short of actual contact, letting her hand hover near his shoulders as he shrugged out of the corduroy, then happily hanging it on one of the hooks by the door among other coats of various sizes and colors. Martin heard classical music playing somewhere, and noticed a pot on the stove was simmering. Maybe there really was chicken soup.

"Sam is upstairs. He'll be so happy to see you—his first real friend in the neighborhood!" She gave him a plate full of Oreos and followed him with two glasses of milk through the dining room and down the hall, reaching forward with a hand that held a glass of milk and tapping his shoulder to give him directions as he tried to hold the plate steady, the cookies nearly sliding off as he made each turn.

"How is school? Sam seems to like it so far, doesn't he? He's very excited about the big state reports. What state did you get? He's researching Delaware."

"I'm North Dakota," Martin said.

"What's their motto?" she asked, concerned and eager. "Delaware's is 'Strong Deeds; Gentle Words' which I think is nice. They were the first state to ratify the Constitution. Does North Dakota have a motto?"

"Now and Forever?" Martin said, certain he was forgetting part of it.

"Really?" She tapped him and gestured up the stairs. The cookies slid forward, but he leveled the plate before any fell. "Mr. Pearlstein will want you to stay for dinner. He's a little sick of Delaware. There must be so many interesting things you're learning about North Dakota!"

Martin hesitated because he had not learned much about North Dakota. When it had been assigned, he had imagined mailing the governor and the North Dakota Chamber of Commerce and finding some student in Bismarck or Fargo to be his pen pal. But, so far, he had not gone beyond the almanac in the school library. He remembered that there was an official state petrified wood.

Perhaps catching his hesitancy, Mrs. Pearlstein dropped the subject, "We're just glad you are in school with Sam. He was very popular in his old school in Queens, but he needs friends now. I hope you will be good friends. How's your mother? Be sure to tell your mother I say hello."

As they got to the top of the stairs, Martin could see Sam in the bathroom. He had the top of the toilet tank off and his hands were in the pale blue porcelain box. Sam could hear water running.

"This thing is still running, Mother," Sam said, pulling his hands from the water and shaking them over the tank. "If I could use Dad's toolbox, I could fix it."

"Your father will work on it when he gets home."

"I can do it."

"He doesn't like you using his tools."

"I only need the wire cutter. Look at this?" Sam said to Martin. "See this chain?" He pulled at a piece of the innards of the toilet tank. "It's supposed to lift this flap, to let the water out." He pulled at the chain and let the rubber flap flop up and down a few times. "So that lets the water out. Then the flap closes and the tank fills up again. But this chain is cut too long,"— he waved the silver line with a quick circle of his hand—"so sometimes it gets tangled under the flap, creating a little space, letting the water keep running out. The tank never fills and the water never stops." Sam continued to flip the chain for demonstration purposes, while splashing water around the inside of the tank. "I could fix this in two seconds with a little wire cutters my father has that my stupid mother won't let me touch because it's some sort of sacred object."

"Don't be rude, Samuel." She tapped his shoulder. "Wash your hands and go eat your cookies."

"Arrghh!" Sam growled and went into his room—slamming the door and then opening it again to let Martin in with the cookies. He took the two glasses of milk from his mother and kicked the door closed.

"Sam?" his mother called through the door.

"Thank you, Mother!" he called back with saccharine sweetness. "It's the little things," he said to Martin.

For the next hour, they played Monopoly and listened to Beatles records. Sam told Martin about his old neighborhood and Martin told Sam what he knew about the kids at school, warning him about bullies while Sam asked about girls.

"The guy you really need to worry about is Jimmy Jordan."

"Julia Levin is in your reading circle, isn't she?"

"Yeah."

"Does that make it harder to concentrate on *Treasure Island?*" Sam laughed.

"My group is reading *Alice in Wonderland*," Martin said, looking down at Ventnor Ave.

"Yeah, I'm afraid to talk to her, too." Sam laughed again and this time Martin laughed. "Don't worry, I think it's normal to be afraid of pretty girls," Sam said, laughing louder.

"It's normal for me," Martin said, smiling, straightening a pair of houses on Marvin Gardens.

Sam jumped up and went to the window. "Here, look at this."

Martin got up and stood next to Sam looking through where he had pulled back the curtains, decorated with baseball team logos. The window looked over the backyards: a crisp carpet of spring green on the Pearlstein side, then, separated by only a short hurricane fence, his family's patch of tan, overgrown grass and a few scraggly dogwood trees trying to bloom. There was a bicycle lying on its side that must have been out there all winter. Martin could see his mother through the kitchen window. She was standing at the counter, looking down at the row of papers, a pencil in her hand. Sam pointed to the pool one yard over, at the Fillmores'.

"That's Kathy Fillmore's house, isn't it?"

"Yeah."

"So, when it gets a little warmer, she'll swim in that pool?" He pointed to the blue tarp, carefully tied over an above-ground pool for the winter. "Does she wear a bikini?"

Martin remembered the hot afternoon the previous summer when Mrs. Fillmore, who also wore a bikini, had invited all the neighborhood kids into the pool and made Kathy, who was in high school and had a boyfriend, serve lemonade. Martin remembered the moisture beading up on the blue plastic cups, the bright green of Kathy's bathing suit and the hot pink of her sunburned belly. He turned away from the pool to look down at his own backyard and smiled shyly.

"Sometimes," he said, almost whispering. "Sometimes they let us use the pool and sometimes Kathy wears a bikini. It's green."

Sam put his palm out flat toward Martin and said "Cool!" as Martin slapped him five.

They stood quietly a moment and Sam turned to look at Martin's backyard.

"How come you never mow your lawn?"

Martin looked to the corner of the yard by the dogwood tree, its white flowers obscuring the lawnmower resting in the spot where it had run out of gas last June. He knew that saying that the lawnmower was out of gas would not be an adequate explanation, but there was no other.

"I don't know," he said.

Sam looked from the lawn to Martin who continued to stare at the lawn, remembering how angry Mr. Fillmore had gotten in August when the tall grass had gone to seed. Sam shrugged and went to the bedroom door, carefully stepping over the Monopoly board.

"Hey Mom! More cookies!"

"Sam?" Mrs. Pearlstein called up.

"Please!"

Sam came back and plopped himself on the floor, studying the board.

"Can we stop?" he asked. "I kind of hate this game."

Martin turned from his ragged backyard to neat rows of houses on Baltic and Ventnor and St. James Place. "I kind of hate it too," he said. "Can I use your bathroom?"

"Yeah, but then let's go outside and play football or something."

"Sure," Martin said.

Before Martin could even move from the window, Sam had grabbed a ball from under his bed and was running down the stairs, yelling to his mother that they were going. "Out!" he said, in response to her question.

Martin took care to direct his urine against the side of the bowl so the sound of his piss was muffled by the porcelain. He tried to pull the flush lever down slowly, in the hopes of minimizing the noise. He washed his hands quickly and then could not decide between a maroon or a blue towel and was finally wiping his hands on his pants when he heard the toilet stop running.

Martin lifted the porcelain lid off the toilet tank and laid it down on the seat as Sam had. Through the still settling water he saw the end of the chain snaking cleanly away from the rubber flap. It had not caught on the lip this time. The toilet had flushed correctly. Martin jiggled the handle to watch the flap stutter, a bit of water escaping each time. He watched as the chain undulated in the slight turbulence around the rubber flap, waving back and forth around the little opening he repeatedly created, until, finally, the slack end of the chain slipped under the flap, causing the gap Sam had been so upset about. Martin waited a moment watching as the level in the tank dropped, bringing the floating ball down and tripping the flow of water on again, the sound babbling like a blue porcelain brook. Quickly, quietly he replaced the top of the toilet tank, wiped his hands on his pants and ran downstairs.

Trump

"Nigger trumps faggot," Andre told Frankie, spitting blood with the words, a twist of handkerchief stuffed into his left nostril, a line of red between the white cloth and his brown nose. They sat with their backs to the graveyard wall, looking out at the Cunningham family tombstone and the lesser stones of James, Meredith, Frederick, and Eleanor in a horizontal line below it, the dates obscured by the uncut grass. Andre used the toe of his black school shoe to pry a small stone free from the dirt, then tossed it at Meredith.

"Every time," Frankie whispered into his knees as he hugged them to his chest. Then, louder, he said "Sorry," stretching out the word in a whiny singsong voice that made everything sound like a question, a voice he already knew Andre hated. Andre was small and weak, but quick of voice, cutting off just enough breath for each word, as if there was not time for dwelling on what was said. It had been that voice, muttering "Asshole" into Frankie's ear, that had drawn him to Andre just an hour after Brother Clark had introduced Andre to the room, Brother's own soft voice barely above silence, as if unaware that he was introducing the first Black kid into Bishop Keenan High School.

That had been just two weeks after Frankie had transferred from public school to become the focus of every Keenan ninth-grader's rage. That rage made manifest an hour after Andre's introduction in the form of Marco Corre shoving Frankie's giant world history text off Frankie's desk, the fat book slamming to the floor just behind Corre's fat ass squeezing up the aisle, the noise reminding the boys in Brother Clark's class to laugh at everything associated with Frankie Agosta. And everyone did laugh, except this new Black kid whose voice bit off insults aimed at Frankie's tormenters directly into Frankie's ear.

Andre's staccato voice was so opposite the slow drawl of self-pity sliding through Frankie's head at that moment that Frankie Agosta fell a little bit in love with Andre Green. That afternoon, as they waited at the same bus stop for two different buses to travel home in two different directions, Frankie felt he owed it to Andre to point out that once the shock of his existence wore off, Andre would replace Frankie as the student most likely to get punched after school.

"You mean nigger trumps faggot?" Andre had asked with a smile that dared Frankie to return it.

"Every time," Frankie smiled.

Andre laughed, a quick spitting sound, and shook his head. "I guess I owe you for the few days of peace then, faggot," and Frankie smiled to hear the word in simple jest.

"What's that?" Andre used his chin to point at the small crowd of boys heading down MacDonald Avenue under the elevated tracks.

Frankie turned away as if casually looking for his bus. "That's Connor Pierce and his crew," Frankie tried to say each word quickly and distinctly, but the long vowels slid together and it seemed to him he was talking too much. "Heading for Perpetual Grace."

"What?"

"The cemetery." Frankie kept his hands in his pockets, pointing at the high, brownstone wall randomly spotted black with soot, just beyond the el with his chin. "They meet girls there. From Sorrow." Frankie shifted his chin toward the yellow brick building beyond the cemetery, about as far north of Perpetual Grace as Keenan was south. Our Lady of the Sorrows: Bishop Keenan's Sister School.

"Girls? In the cemetery?"

"That's what I hear. It's all big kids, seniors. We can't go."

"Why can't we go?" Andre laughed, putting his arm around Frankie's neck, drawing him toward MacDonald Avenue. "You look kind of dead."

"If Connor Pierce sees us," Frankie said, just slightly less afraid than he was thrilled, "we'll both be dead."

Andre skipped ahead and Frankie had to walk slowly to force Andre to stay back until the lanky upperclassmen, their ties undone and their blazers stuffed into their bookbags climbed over the brownstone wall. Andre waited on the sidewalk while Frankie stood in the afternoon shadow the wall threw and watched as the long arms and legs scrambled up the brown stone, with Connor Pierce pausing atop the wall, beating his chest like a gorilla and shouting out, "Nicolette!" The sight of Connor—who was in Frankie's gym class and liked to punch people at random—always made Frankie short of breath.

Andre convinced Frankie to climb the wall and jump down from the six feet of brown stone to the weedy patch of grass where their bravado wore off. Just ahead, past the Cunningham plot, past the D'Andrea's guardian angel, there was small hill and beyond that there were girls. Juniors, seniors and a few bold younger termers. The quiet hills and clean grass of the cemetery brought boys in white polyester shirts and blue ties and girls in heather gray skirts and tight blue pull-up socks, to circle and flirt and occasionally pair off.

Or so Frankie and Andre imagined. Though from that day on they went almost every afternoon, they never ventured past the Cunningham plot and spent most of their time sitting in the weeds against that wall, the brown dust of the stones rubbing into their white shirts as they wondered both aloud and silently what might be happening on the other side of that hill. Andre spoke mostly of Sondra Washington, a tall, bony, brown-skinned girl, almost a foot taller than Andre, but with his same quick laugh and nervous, skipping walk. She was Andre's counterpart, the first Black girl at Sorrow. Frankie did not think of any particular girl, but of girls as a category, an abstract threat hovering in his future. He thought of his mother walking back and forth through the house, her heels clicking with various timbers on the lino-leum, wood, and carpeted floors so that everyone always knew what room she was worrying in. He held his breath and imagined that beyond the hill the boys and girls were breathing freely, laughing, loosely relaxed in a way he had never been with anyone, moving among each other without fear.

Taking off your jacket and tie before you got home, tres-passing in the cemetery, being seen with Sorrow girls, all of it was against the rules, but the only person who might be interested in such a crime was Father Brennan, the principal of Bishop Keenan who sometimes reached out to kids with no friends, kids that got picked on, the wimps and geeks and faggots. He would often come up behind such boys as they sat alone in the cafeteria, put his hands on their shoulders and say something loud about God's grace and the lonely life of those who follow Christ.

"He's a pasty-faced faggot himself," Andre said. "He was in the meeting with my mom when they let me in this fucking school." Andre tossed a stone at Meredith Cunningham's grave. "He slid his chair right up so our knees were touching and said all this shit about turning the other cheek," Andre spoke with palpable disgust. "He kept bringing up Martin Luther King and touching my wrist. His breath smelled like fish. Before we left he made us all hold hands and pray."

Andre shuddered. "I thought my father was going to punch the guy."

Frankie's father, Mr. Agosta, also disliked Father B. One Sunday, Frankie and his dad rode in Mr. Agosta's Oldsmobile to get a quart of lemon ice on New Utrecht Avenue. Mr. Zacharia, who owned the store, but spent all day on the sidewalk talking up the passerby while a Puerto Rican kid ran the counter and bussed the tables, always greeted Mr. Agosta, with a kiss on the cheek, then pretended to punch Frankie in the stomach. They got the ices and *The Daily News* and Mr. Agosta got cigarettes. Frankie got gum, to hide the smell of the cigarettes he would steal from his father later. Returning home, they had the usual trouble finding parking, and had to squeeze in next to a bus stop on 65th Street. When Frankie opened the passenger door, Mr. Agosta put an arm out and held him in his seat.

"We need to talk."

Frankie thought his father had learned that he was failing gym and dreaded the hours at the basketball courts the man would prescribe, heaving the ball up at the rim in the fading light while his father shouted instructions and encouragement and his mother waited dinner, looking out the window at the dusk, ringing her hands.

Mr. Agosta coughed, covering his mouth with a loose fist.

"Your mother thinks we should talk about sex."

Frankie waited.

"You don't have any questions, do you?"

Frankie paused for a moment, then muttered dryly, "No."

"You know it was her idea. To put you in that school. Catholic school. You know that wasn't my idea."

Frankie waited.

"I respect your mother's beliefs. She has a right to believe." Mr. Agosta ran a hand down his face, pulling his cheeks out of line with his mouth. "But you have to admit. Those priests. Father Brennan. It's an odd life." He stared out the window at the traffic on 65th Street. "I'm not fully comfortable with him being the one. To teach this. So, if you have any questions. Girls. Anything."

Frankie waited as his father stared out at the traffic.

"You come to me. It's natural for a father and son. To talk." And Mr. Agosta reached over and tousled Frankie's hair as he had done when Frankie was a boy, then got out of the car and gestured toward the back seat.

"Frankie, grab those packages."

The day after Connor pulled Frankie's shorts down on the basketball court during gym, sneaking up behind him while Frankie was guarding Mike Dwyer, getting hold of Frankie's gym shorts and his Fruit of the Looms in one swift pull so that Frankie bounced up and down for all to see, nearly falling over as he tripped about, trying to pull up his shorts and stop Dwyer who drove past him for an easy layup, Father B called Frankie into the office.

First, Father B came to Brother Clark's class. Usually, he came bursting in, moving Brother out of the way and writing "L-O-V-E" or "P-E-A-C-E" in giant letters across the board while boys sniggered, then asking the class what that meant with the correct answer usually being "God" or "Jesus" but sometimes "The Holy Spirit." This time he opened the door quietly, scanning the room and letting his gaze rest on Connor, then looking at Frankie and smiling.

"Francis Martin Agosta, please come to my office."

When Frankie got out into the hallway, Father B was gone, so Frankie walked very slowly to his office and knocked very softly. Inside there was a desk and a picture of the Pope and a bookshelf loaded down with papers and folded up banners. There were two chairs in front of the desk Father B sat behind, but one had a pile of papers on it so Frankie sat in the other and coughed into his tightly clenched fist.

After another few moments of studying the calendar on his desk, turning the pages back and forth and counting, Father B put the calendar away in a drawer and looked up.

"How are you, Francis?"

"Fine, Father."

"Have you recovered from yesterday?"

Then Frankie knew why he was there.

"Yesterday? You mean the Global History quiz? I did OK on that."

Father B frowned, pursing his lips as if Frankie had cursed.

After a moment of silence, Father B continued. "You know, Francis, being singled out for attention is not a bad thing, even if the particular form of attention has negative qualities."

"Yes, Father." Frankie's eyes wandered down to the papers on the chair next to him.

"Even negative, unwanted attention like getting picked on or bullied can have its own sort of grace."

"Yes, Father." Frankie noticed that the papers were last week's religion exam on the sacraments, already graded. The top paper belonged to George Carroll. He had gotten an 83. There was a long pause here as Father B sat looking at Frankie and Frankie sat looking at George Carroll's test paper. Both had their hands in their laps. After a long silence, Frankie repeated,

"Yes, Father."

"When Connor pulled your shorts down in gym," the words rushed from Father B as if he were himself embarrassed by them, "There is a grace even in that. Do you know what that grace is?"

"No, Father."

"Forgiveness," Father B tapped lightly on the surface of his desk with the flat of his hand, bringing the hand down softly and then letting it hover over the surface as he continued. "When you forgave those boys for laughing, when you turned the other cheek…"

Frankie looked up at Father B, thinking that he was being laughed at again, but Father B was looking back softly, the acceptance and caring in his eyes appeared genuine.

"You, Francis Martin Agosta, achieved a kind of grace."

Frankie wondered about telling Father B that he had not forgiven Connor or Dwyer or Coach Calender, who ran his class as if the very point of gym was for jocks to torment faggots. He glanced back down at George Carroll's paper. George had gotten Extreme Unction wrong on the multiple choice. Frankie thought he, too, had put 'B: Epiphany.'

"People who can forgive those who trespass against them," Father B came out from behind his desk and sat on its front edge, one foot up on the seat of Frankie's chair, between Frankie's knees. "They are already doing God's work."

Frankie sat up straighter, moving his face and chest further from that leg, pressing his shoulders against the straight chair back.

"Yes, Father."

There was a long awkward moment of silence and Father B kept looking at Frankie and Frankie nervously searched the room for something to look at. Pope Paul was looking down at him and George Carroll's B- was looking up at him and Father B's knee was directly in front of him. Frankie stared at the desk beyond Father B's knee, noticing that light lines of grain stood out against the dark wood. The lines were waving in an almost parallel pattern across the surface. After a long moment, Frankie repeated "Yes, Father," and Father B smiled.

"Back to class," he said, but before Frankie could slide out of the narrow space Father B put his hand on Frankie's shoulder and whispered dramatically "I want you to think about that grace, Francis. What does it mean in your life?"

"Do you ever move any faster?" Andre said, skipping ahead and turning to walk backwards and plead for Frankie to

hurry up. Frankie walked no faster, but turned around to see if anyone was behind them.

Once at the cemetery wall, they waited, sharing a cigarette Frankie had stolen from his father. Andre pushed off the wall and looked toward New Utrecht from time to time, while Frankie stayed in the shadow, keeping an eye out for the older boys on 14th Avenue.

"Maybe she's not coming," Frankie said.

"Of course, she's coming," Andre laughed. "There's only two of us in the whole neighborhood—we might as well enjoy each other's company."

"That is so racist," Frankie said.

"Shut up, faggot," Andre laughed and pushed Frankie against the wall, just as Sondra came around one corner and Connor and Marco came around the other.

"You gonna let this nigger call you faggot?" Connor flicked a finger at Frankie's eyebrow, snapping him on the bone of his eye socket. Frankie flinched, partly in pain, and partly in fear of the loud snap, of the hand coming up at his face. "Huh?" Connor said, standing close enough that Frankie could taste him in the air, a mix of sweat and Brut in the back of his throat. Connor flicked his finger again, hitting the red mark made the first time, stinging Frankie's eye and making his vision go blurry. "You really must be a faggot. Visiting with Father B?" Connor sang in a high-pitched whine that mimicked Frankie's own. "Did you offer each other a sign of peace?"

Connor flicked a third time and Frankie thought his eye would pop out of its socket, and he wrenched his shoulder free of Connor's grasp and turned to the wall to hide his shame and tears. Connor and Marco walked past, shoving Andre aside, and approached Sondra who was waiting, pretending not to watch, chatting with a short busty girl.

Faggot had nothing to do with sex, Frankie told himself, seeing Connor lean his arm against the wall of the cemetery, his face close to Sondra's as Marco and the short busty girl stood ignoring each other. Sondra laughed, but ducked under Connor's arm to continue walking. Connor reached out to touch her and she shrugged him off, turning and putting her hand up like a traffic cop, palming him into place. Connor thrust his arms out at either side, like he was pleading with her, but Sondra laughed again, shaking her head and turning to walk back around New Utrecht out of sight. The short busty girl smiled at Marco, shrugged her shoulders, and followed Sondra.

Frankie shrank back against the wall, but Andre stood on the sidewalk, smiling as Connor and Marco walked back past.

"Fuck you, nigger," Connor spat, punching Andre with a short, sharp right fist. Andre's nose burst bloody and he slumped against the wall. Frankie froze as if at attention as the two older boys walked away. Then he pulled a wad of wrinkled handkerchief out of his pocket and handed it to Andre. Sondra and her friend appeared again from New Utrecht walking toward them.

"Fuck me," Andre muttered, and boosted himself up, black leather shoes scuffling over the stones as the two boys scrambled over the wall and onto the grass at the foot of the Cunningham family.

"You got flicked on the cheek," Andre complained, wiping at the blood on his white shirt. "I got a bloody nose."

"Sorry," Frankie moaned.

"You don't have to be sorry," Andre said, folding Frankie's handkerchief, now streaked with rusty bloodstains, and returning it to him, "You need to stay away from Father B."

"I know," Frankie muttered, speaking into his knees, which were folded up at his chin, then, even quieter, whispering another apology. He slipped the handkerchief into his blazer pocket and felt Andre's shoulder touching his as they leaned against the wall. Faggot, he told himself, had nothing to do with sex.

"We got enough trouble without his help," Andre warned.

Frankie knew that Andre was right, but could think of no alternative when, on Thursday, Father B asked Frankie back into the office. This time the test papers were gone and Father B sat next to Frankie.

"Francis, God's mystery is difficult to unfold. Some would say it is impossible, and for too many people, I fear that is true." Father B put a hand on the back of Frankie's chair. "We should think with kindness of those who will live outside of God's grace, outside looking in."

Frankie did not look at Father Brennan, but studied the grain of wood on his desk, following the lines that started off parallel and then mixed and merged as they made their way across the wood. Frankie studied the wood but kept his mind focused on Father B's hands. One was resting on Father's knee, which was poking Frankie because Father B was twisted around in his chair to face Frankie. Frankie wondered how he would react if Father B touched him. He was aware of the door beyond Father B and all the boys in the hallway beyond that door. He knew those boys were ready to laugh at him, to pull a jockstrap down over his face, to throw milk cartons at him in the cafeteria, or who knew what else if they saw him here in this office with this man's soft, cool voice and a hand on the back of his chair and a bit of talcum powder at the edge of his collar.

"It's not unusual for those called to Jesus's service to know the call very young. I knew when I was your age, and I was guided by men who saw that grace in me and nurtured it."

On the word "nurtured," Father B put his palm gently on Frankie's knee, touching him for a brief second, then letting the hand hover above Frankie's chinos. Frankie closed his eyes.

"Do you know when I saw that grace in you, Francis?"

"In the gym last week?" Frankie felt his face getting hot, felt the shame return. He thought he might throw up.

"No, that was when I realized that the flame in you, that spark, needed help or it would flicker and die." The palm of Father B's hand came down for another gentle second on Frankie's knee. Frankie closed his eyes tighter.

"I first saw that flickering light of God's grace in you when Andre Green came to Bishop Keenan. All of us were challenged to accept this Negro boy as a child of God and, as you know, some of us have failed. Even among the faculty, some have had a hard time opening our hearts to the boy."

Frankie opened his eyes now and saw the grain of Father B's desk, swirling together again.

"Among the students … well, you have seen better than I."

Frankie saw the lines gather themselves into a knot at the corner.

"Yet you have reached out to him. You have offered him the hand of friendship. You have offered him sanctuary."

Frankie imagined the knot dissolving, on the other side of the desk, where he couldn't see it, the grains becoming individual lines again. Frankie stood up and Father B followed, putting both hands on Frankie's shoulders.

"Your willingness to befriend the weakest among us shows you have a special ability to love. And here in this office, I am offering you the same sanctuary you have offered little Andre Green."

Frankie moved a hand into his blazer pocket and felt the soft cloth of his bloody handkerchief. He remembered the cold air of the gym on his crotch and thighs, the sting of Connor's fingers against his cheekbone and the heat of his tears. He squeezed past Father B, slipping under the hands on his shoulders and opening the door. He could see boys leaning against lockers, boys rushing toward the gym, boys just standing in the halls between classes. Connor and Marco came out of Brother Dunleavy's math class; Andre was right behind them. All three looked first at Frankie and then at Father B, smiling in the door behind him, his hand on Frankie's shoulder again.

"Anytime," Father B said, in a voice loud enough to be heard by every boy in the hall. "Come see me anytime."

"Sanctuary," Frankie mumbled as he crossed the hall. Connor did not dare flick at his ear or smack the back of his head or pull his pants up until his crotch hurt while Father B was watching, so Frankie was able to slip past Connor and step right up to Andre.

Andre said "Hey," but raised one eyebrow and leaned his head back so that his chin pointed through Frankie's chest and on toward Father B still standing in his office door, as if to silently ask, "What gives?"

In answer, Frankie made a fist and punched Andre quick and sharp, feeling his knuckles crush Andre's thick lips against his healthy white teeth, following through so that Andre's head snapped backwards and he stumbled back into math class, knocking over a desk as he fell to the floor.

Frankie turned and walked away. He could hear Connor and Marco laughing, but he could no longer hear Father B calling his name, suddenly, in anger.

Manifest Destiny

Cars and front lawns were important currency on Long Island, so the long, seedy stalks that made our front lawn look like a Nebraska wheat farm would have been enough to make us unpopular with our neighbors even if the driveway hadn't held that Buick. This was the late '70s, so we're talking about a car the size of a small apartment. My father—having lost the company car when he lost his job—had bought it used. Really used. A faded black convertible with splits in the red upholstery, a cracked windshield, and a muffler held on with wire, that car was the bully I cowered in fear of. The brakes squealed when my mother dropped me off at school; dark smoke poured out of the tail pipe during my driving test; I drove Rosemary Pollack to the prom, but she got a ride home with someone else.

Maybe the worst thing about that car was its perpetually unfulfilled promise of imminent breakdown, an event I wished for every spring on the train home from Boston. But it was still there, parked beside the ragged brown grass, when I graduated. When I had moved my stuff back into the bedroom with the posters of Farrah Fawcett and Blue Öyster Cult, I went downstairs and offered to take the car to the shop, get the muffler replaced.

Or I could mow the lawn, I suggested, careful to keep any tone of judgment out of my voice.

My father glared at my betrayal. We don't worry about things like that, he said. Cars are supposed to make noise. Grass is supposed to grow. We only worry when they stop.

When he first got laid off, the iconoclasm of his reaction had seemed endearing. He would hold court in the father's corner at barbecues and birthday parties, condemning the ratrace; arguing that the golf course at the end of our block should be a public park. Since, like all the other men in that circle, he had bought a house on California Street because it dead-ended on the tenth hole—proof that he was winning the ratrace—his lectures were met with an amused head shake, a pat on the back, an assurance that things would get better. But when he stopped mowing the lawn so it could reseed naturally, the arguments heated up. Then, when that car roared into the driveway, we stopped getting invited to those barbecues.

So while my father wore his old suits with t-shirts and sandals, shuffling between the TV and the liquor cabinet, I spent my days sending out resumes. I answered every want ad, not caring what job it advertised. I would be a salesman, a paralegal, a journalist. Hell, a beggar man thief. I just wanted to go somewhere else, be someone else.

Meanwhile, I had a lot of time on my hands and no particular place to go. I was home for dinner every night, listening to my father lecture about the mindless conformity swallowing America while my mother stamped her cigarette out in her baked potato and worried about the electric bill.

The only escape was that car. In acknowledgment of its lack of value, the keys were kept in the ignition and every night I would try to leave quietly, giving one burst of noisy gas, then coasting to the stop sign before gunning the engine, letting the rumble drown my embarrassment as I headed out to Sunrise Highway. I drove east, passing each identical town, until the last one disappeared behind me, and I crossed into the dark farm country out beyond Babylon and Bay Shore.

I'd pull over next to some empty field and watch the moth-like stars flickering in the too-dark sky until I was sure my parents had gone to sleep, then make a U-turn and drive back west, past those identical towns, each with its own shoe store and supermarket, hobby shop and diner.

One night, after watching Robert Mitchum on the 4:30 movie, I put on a seersucker jacket that I thought made me look older, forced the top on that convertible down and let the engine roar like a fighter jet into the parking lot of that little strip mall on Brower Avenue. All three stores were open late, and I passed Grayfield Pharmacy and Max's Deli to enter Frank's Liquors for the first time in my life. There were shelves to the ceiling of wines and liquors arranged by color and country, and I stood there wondering which bottle contained liquid strong and sharp enough to cut through the taste of sleeping in the same bed where I had reached puberty until the man playing the part of Frank looked up from his little black and white TV, pushed a pint of Jack Daniels across the counter at me and rang up the purchase.

As I came out, trying to fit the brown paper bag into the pocket of my jacket, a clutch of teenagers, two guys and a girl, stepped from the shadows. They were maybe sixteen, but the kid who stepped up into the light had beautifully scruffy hair and a sneering Jim Morrison impersonation.

Hey man, buy us some beer? He held out a fist full of dollar bills.

I hesitated. I wasn't really a moralist about such things, but it was a residential neighborhood, just these three stores on the corner surrounded by front doors and two car garages. I looked around at all those neatly trimmed lawns shaming me.

C'mon he said. Be cool. His voice implied the sort of cosmic bond I had never achieved with the cool kids in high school, and it occurred to me that if I were his age he wouldn't give me the time of day.

Hey Marty, the girl said, and, when she stepped into the light, I realized I knew her. Little Athena Futterman from next door. I had not seen her in a few years. I remembered she had been a cute kid—skinny and fierce in her soccer uniform, always running somewhere. Her father was a dentist who told everyone what to do. She was something beyond cute now—slim and long-legged, with glimmering blonde hair. She smiled.

Athena, I said. Hi. How've you been?

Cool, she said. Everything's cool. Just trying to get a little beer buzz, and, keeping her hands in the pockets of her cut-offs, she shrugged one shoulder toward the hand clutching the dollar bills—a movement that caused her t-shirt to slip, revealing the white strap of a bra.

You know each other? The boy with the bills turned on the full rock star wattage of his smile. Cool, man.

Yeah, I sighed. OK, and put out my hand for the bills.

Two sixpacks, he said. And none of that Miller High Life shit. Michelob.

I nodded and tried to jimmy the math in my head, but couldn't make her older than sixteen.

Paul rang up the purchase, craning his neck to watch Athena and the boys loitering on the sidewalk. Take it around the corner, he said. Mr. Carmichael don't like you giving it to kids right in front of the store. I hefted the brown paper bag. And don't get caught, he warned.

Outside, I gestured toward the parking lot and walked that way. All three of them followed me around the corner, out of sight of the store's plate glass front and neon signs. When they caught up, I simply put the bag down on the blacktop and backed away toward my car, watching Athena watch Morrison inspect the beer.

Very cool, Morrison said. Thanks. He bent over, reached down into the bag and pulled out a brown-and-gold bottle. You want one?

Now I lifted the brown paper bag an inch or two from my pocket, trying to make my smile small and knowing. I was slightly ashamed at this obvious pandering to a teenager, but Athena smiled back when I did it.

Cooool man, the kid said, stretching out the word and nodding like he really meant it.

I had just started my car when the flashing lights appeared, the short burst of siren like a horn section to the bass of my engine. I watched through the windshield as the police pulled up and got out, cutting off the escape for the two boys, and saw that, somehow, Athena had separated herself, hung back while the boys stashed bottles in every conceivable pocket and then, maybe seeing the police a second before the rest of us, turned and followed me to the car. Because the top was down, she didn't need to open the door, just turned her back to the car, pressed the seat of her Jordache cut-offs against that top edge where the window was rolled down, and, lifting her legs, spun herself into the passenger seat.

Can we go? she asked, her voice nervously polite.

As I pulled away, the cops looked up at the roar of my engine but both of them had their hands full of the bottles so they just shook their heads as I pulled onto the street.

Fucking pigs, she said. I want to say it was under her breath, but it must have been louder if I heard it over the engine. I didn't say anything until we had cut over to Long Beach Road and were stopped at a red light.

Where are we going? I asked. I was confused, unused to driving with anyone else in the car.

She was smiling wide now. I love the beach, she said, and settled back into the seat.

I nodded, put on my turn signal, and headed south.

I like convertibles, she said, pretending she didn't have to shout and tossing her hair behind her and up, into the wind.

We didn't talk much more in the car, enveloped in the rushing air and the noise of the engine. I kept thinking of the difference between sixteen and twenty-two and didn't look at her again until she let out a whooping squeal and threw her arms up as we pulled into the parking lot at Point Lookout. The beach was closed, of course, but in those days no one bothered you. I parked a few spaces away from a pickup truck with a camper shell covering the bed, fishing poles and buckets and assorted gear visible through the sliding back windows. When I turned off the ignition, the silence wrapped around us like salt air.

It was cool for mid-August and as we walked out toward the point, I wished for a moment that I had been someone else in high school, that I was someone else now. Athena took off her shoes and ran ahead, her long legs easily outpacing me. She stopped at the last lifeguard station and climbed the up wooden ladder. I climbed up and sat facing her, the two of us leaning against opposite sides of the wide bench.

Athena reached one leg across and tapped at my jacket with her sandal, pink, painted toes pushing the bottle against my hip. Are you going to open that?

I took out the paper bag and unscrewed the bottle's cap, that firm click as the seal broke. The first sip burned my throat and I choked back a cough, feeling the tears leak from my eyes. I realized why I had never had whiskey before. I was going to put it away, but Athena reached over and took the bottle from my hand.

Her first sip was bigger than mine and she did not bother to choke back her cough. Her face turned red and she shook her head so that the light reflected in waves off her blonde hair. She sucked in air and laughed at herself. Wow, she said. That is not Budweiser. But when she got control of her breathing, she took another sip, her hair shaking only slightly as she shivered the drink down.

Take it easy, I said.

It's nice out here, she said, sitting back and looking around. I've never been here at night.

We sat under the stars and looked out at the dark ocean. The sky was only distinguishable from the water by the thin gray lines of surf breaking somewhere offshore. I leaned against my side of the bench and she leaned against hers. We passed the bottle back and forth. She wasn't more than sixteen but out-sipped me two to one; I concentrated on making sure our legs didn't touch.

So, who were those guys? I asked.

Ray and Herb? she said, then shrugged. Boys.

Will they be mad at you for—I stopped, searching for the right word.

Ditching? she said, laughing lightly. Who would have stayed?

She sipped again, held the paper-bag-encased bottle between her knees. Maybe a little. Mad. But they're boys. She tossed her hair over one shoulder, passed me the bottle. They get mad. It passes. I'm used to it.

I guess you can get used to anything, I said, just to fill the silence really. I squeezed the bottle in one hand, feeling the hard glass beneath the brown paper before putting it to my lips, letting a trickle wash hot and sharp over my tongue.

I know you can get used to anger, she said, her voice suddenly sharp, pointed. Live with my dad, you'd better get used to it.

Dr. Futterman had broad shoulders, close-cropped black curls, and a deep, demanding voice. I had heard him yelling in the house and I remembered him threatening to get up a petition if my father didn't cut the grass. He was like the mayor of the block. I wasn't sure if I should say any of that. My father has a temper, too, I offered.

Athena reached out and took the bottle from me, then gestured with it, pointing the mouth at me as she spoke. But your father's cool. She took an enthusiastic pull at the bottle. He doesn't get angry over stupid shit. He's like, angry at the world. Righteous.

I guess, I said. Until the world gets angry back.

Fuck the world, she said, sipping gently this time.

The whole world? I asked.

And what's with that car? Athena laughed.

I shrugged. It runs, I said, repeating what he always said, shame clogging my throat.

It sure does, she said, then laughed and made a deep rustling sound with her voice, trying to imitate the muffler. She sipped from the bottle and when I reached for it took another quick swallow before handing it over to me. It got us this far, she shrugged.

Maybe you should take it easy on this stuff? I said, then put the bottle to my mouth, keeping my lips closed, only pretending to drink.

She laughed, reached out and took back the bottle, nearly empty now.

Yeah, your dad's cool. He does not give a half a fuck about what anybody says. That's the way to be.

You think? I asked, watching her look out at the ocean. I don't know. I think it's OK to get along, fit in.

NO! Athena scolded, gesturing at me with the brown-bagged bottle. I don't want to fit in. I don't need people telling me I'm pretty. It wasn't even my idea to be a cheerleader!

I didn't know you were a cheerleader, I said. Congratulations.

I don't want to lead anyone, she said. I just want to go my own way. Away from here. Far away. She sipped again, then shook the bottle and handed it to me, finally empty. She stared out at the dark, focused on the invisible horizon. What's out there? She asked. Europe? I wish we could just walk to Europe. Or Paris! Wouldn't that be cool? If we could just walk to Paris? She pointed out to the invisible horizon, her voice so full of longing I didn't have the heart to tell her we were facing south and would end up in Bermuda, maybe the Dominican Republic. I want to get to that place, she said, where people can't tell me what to do. Who to be.

I thought about the mailbox, the letter I was waiting for—someone, anyone, telling me what to do, who to be.

Let's you and me do something crazy, she said. Right now. Something no one would expect.

Crazier than this? I asked, holding up the empty bottle in its brown paper wrapping. I looked at where that t-shirt had slipped off her shoulder and quickly looked away. I think maybe we should go home.

Swimming! she said, throwing her arms out as if this were some new way to embrace the universe, the sand, the stars, the surf.

Swimming? I looked up the beach for those fishermen, You mean skinny dipping? I asked, terrified at whatever she might say.

She looked up in surprise, her eyes wide like she was seeing me for the first time, then threw her shoulders back and ratcheted her voice back to confidence. You do what you want, she said. But this is just like a bathing suit, and she pulled her t-shirt over her head, revealing a plain white bra; nothing lacy or lowcut, but let's face it, a bra.

She tossed the shirt down to the sand and turned to climb after it. It was only then that I realized how drunk she was—one foot on the top rung of the ladder, an arm clinging to the back of the bench as she swung crazily over the side, her free arm and leg waving in the dark, her body spinning too far before she called out in riotous laughter and fell to the sand.

I jumped down to see if she was alright. She was lying on the sand, her arms spread out like she was making snow angels, her legs bent underneath her in a way that scared me until she pushed them out in front of her and held out her hands for me to pull her up.

Come on! We're going swimming!

But when our hands touched, her face panicked, her eyes rolled up into their lids and she turned over on her side and threw up, her stomach heaving twice, three times, the whiskey pouring back out of her darkly fouled by whatever she'd had had for dinner. I dropped to my knees beside her and touched her shoulder. Are you alright? She curled into a ball, pulling that shoulder away from me and spit, trying to clear her mouth, then moaned once and dry-heaved.

There was vomit on her cheek and the straight blonde of her hair was now clumped together by a pasty mixture of sand and bile.

She moaned.

I wished that I had some water and looked toward the dark gray lines of surf, but realized right away that was the wrong direction. I bent down and grabbed her by the shoulders, her skin warm to the touch, and pulled her to sitting upright. Sit up, I said. Just stay there. I found her t-shirt in the sand. Her face was vacant and staring as I pulled it back over her head, but when my hand, up under her shirt to push her arm through the sleeve, brushed against the cup of her bra, she shoved me away and put the other arm through herself. I stood up and took a step back from her, held out a hand to pull her to her feet, only to have her slap my hand away.

Can you get up? Walk? I asked, draping my jacket over her shoulders, a chivalrous gesture that only made her look smaller, more defeated.

She looked up at me disdainfully. Of course I can walk, she said, then stumbled and would have fallen if I had not put my forearm under her armpit and lifted her, guiding her back through the sand, the beach grass on the dunes, to the blacktop of the parking lot.

A man was packing that truck, an 8-foot surf-casting rod leaning against the tailgate. He held a large silver fish by the gills and was feeding the tail into the Budweiser cooler on the tailgate. He stopped briefly and looked at us, one hand holding the head of the fish high, the other pushing things around inside the cooler, ice or leftover beer or whatever, making room. I imagined we looked suspicious—a man propping up a teenage girl, drunk and disheveled, against the side of his car while he fumbled for the keys. I was afraid he'd come over to say something, check on us, but he looked nervous himself and began to move more quickly, hurrying to get away.

Do you want to throw up again? I asked Athena.

She shook her head. I never wanted to throw up, she said.

I mean, do you think you can get in the car?

Oh yeah. I'm getting in the car.

Right, right, I said, opening the passenger door—it was a two-door car so the passenger door was long and heavy and I had to shift Athena back toward the trunk and then take her under the arm again and steer her into the front seat.

I didn't want to look at the fisherman, running around his truck and tying poles and nets to his roof rack, but, after I started the car and the engine gunned like a jet plane, I had to turn in that direction to pull out of the parking space. He had stopped and was staring at me, like he could see the noise, then craned his neck to watch me maneuver toward the exit.

The air was colder on the way home—Athena huddled under my jacket like it was a blanket, the wind at least blowing some of the sand and vomit out of her hair as it whipped across her face, her head lolled back, her eyes staring blankly toward the sky. I wondered if she were crying.

Are you OK? I asked.

Just drive.

Right, I said. I'm driving.

The sky and the roads were both clear and we rode a long string of yellow lights, each intersection snapping to red just as I crossed through it, four miles back to Rockville Centre.

We were passing the darkened liquor store when I finally said, Don't worry, I know where you live.

She didn't laugh.

Our neighborhood was just a series of dead ends pressed against the golf course, each street just a few identical houses with a view of a fairway. First Missouri, then blocks labeled Kansas and Oklahoma, Texas, New Mexico, and Arizona. I drove to the one at the end—California, obviously. Split level houses on either side, then just a yellow warning sign, a fence, and the green grass and sand traps beyond that.

As I turned the corner, the car seemed to respond with an especially focused roar, followed by a sudden sharp, crack and a new, uncomfortable silence. I coasted up the block past my house with its amber waves of grain and every light burning and let the car stop in front of Athena's where the windows were dark, pale gray shades pulled down across each of them. There was a new Mercedes in the driveway I was now blocking.

My father's pride and joy, Athena said, her breath fogging the window her head leaned against.

Yeah, I joked, tapping the steering wheel. Mine, too.

She opened the door and shoved it out as if she needed a wide berth to exit.

Are your parents home? I asked. Will you get in trouble?

Don't worry, she mumbled. If I get up for SAT prep tomorrow, no one will even know.

But you'll be alright? I asked. Do you want me to walk you—

Just go, she said, pushing herself to standing on the strip of lawn between the street and the sidewalk and slamming the door shut before she slouched toward the front of her house.

I had forgotten to take back my jacket and I was struck by how little girlish she looked in that oversized seersucker, her legs thin, childlike. At the front door, Athena stopped and looked back at me, her face blank. She was waiting for me to leave, shift to reverse and roar backwards to my own house, but the noise was gone—it would take a tow truck to move that car now. I pictured my father, still up, pacing the living room, listening to the silence. A slight breeze slid past my ears, the seeded tops of our grass stirring in the wind. I gave Athena a little wave, lifting the four fingers off the steering wheel. Then she went through that front door and I turned forward to face the dead end, the fence, the closely trimmed fairway beyond.

Even Richard Nixon

The F train was stuck just outside of the Smith Street station, high above the Gowanus; the stench of the canal—which had once meant jobs but was now just stench—enveloped the rush hour crowd I was now part of. I was not quite rushing to my first job—research assistant for a law firm that needed very little assistance. Pressing my face against the glass of the subway door, I could look down on the roof of my building at the cheap lawn chair I had dragged up for Fourth of July, the plate full of melted candle wax still sitting on the tar paper.

As the train pulled into Borough Hall, passengers emerged from their heat-induced haze and moved toward the door. I allowed the flow of hot bodies to carry me off the train toward the IRT. A young woman I had gone on a blind date with ran past without recognizing me, the lapels on her blouse flapping in the breeze of her movements. She squeezed through the closing doors of the train I had just left, got a seat, and pulled a magazine out of her handbag.

It was almost August and Manhattan was deep into the slush of summer. By the time I reached Redd, Root, and Lavarr, Attorneys at Law, I was sweating like a marathon runner. Murlowe had the air conditioner up full blast and the sudden noise and cold was like entering another dimension. Frank Murlowe, head of Legal Research, actually all of legal research, was pounding away at a Selectric typewriter. He wore a spotless white suit, a gray shirt, and a pink bowtie. A row of freshly sharpened pencils bounced up and down lightly on his desk. My desk, empty but for a lone yellow pad, pressed against his so that when I collapsed into my chair, we were facing each other, or would have been in Murlowe had looked up.

Mr. Oakley always knocked on the door and paused before coming in, so I had a chance to grab one of Murlowe's pencils and appear to be writing something on the yellow pad before the door flew open. TJ Oakley, Attorney at Law, was a large man with a five o'clock shadow at ten in the morning and the confidence of one who felt being in charge was his birthright. He clapped his hands twice and bellowed like he was coaching a football team.

"Monday morning gentlemen, so I need paper! The American Legal System runs on paper! The Pecola briefs are ready? I've got lawyers to deal with."

Murlowe pushed a stack of papers across his desk and patted the top of the pile. He avoided eye contact with Oakley in a way that seemed alternately dismissive and obedient. This combination of passivity and arrogance had kept him locked in this backroom since he himself got out of Brooklyn Law six years earlier. That and the fact that he was Black. Oakley may have looked intimidating in his tailored suits and pinkie ring, but he often had to read Murlowe's work twice in order to understand it. Together they made one complete and successful lawyer: a smart and capable person who appeared smart and capable.

Oakley swept up the papers and turned to walk out. Just before closing the door behind him, he called back to Murlowe: "Good work, Otis. Sorry for the crazy weekend."

As the door closed, Murlowe reached across the Selectric and took the pencil out of my hand. He placed it back in the row of twelve on his desk, straightened the entire group, and returned to his typing.

"You should fire that guy," I swiveled my chair around to the coffee machine and poured myself a cup, covering its surface with white powdered creamer. "Let him try to get anything done without you."

"Even you must have noticed that it doesn't work that way." Murlowe mumbled.

"Yeah, well, Come the Revolution," I said, putting my feet up on the desk and raising my coffee cup in salute.

"Come the Revolution," Murlowe answered, his voice flat and quiet.

"So, what happened this weekend?" I asked. "Why is the big man apologizing?"

"I worked on the Pecola brief." Murlowe answered, picking up one of his pencils and tapping the desk as he read over his latest page of typing. "My trusted assistant got drunk and got laid."

"Unfortunately, you are only half right," I sighed, picking up another of Murlowe's pencils and sketching a portrait of my mug on the yellow pad. "But you work every weekend, and I… I don't." I drew the steam of hot coffee rolling above the mug. "What made this one different?"

"Don't you even read the papers?" Murlowe spoke to the paper in his typewriter. "I mean I understand that legal research is not in your future, but I would think you would make it past page 6 of the *Post*."

I began working the eddies of smoke into a portrait of Murlowe, his face blank with concentration. He typed.

"Nixon?" I asked.

Murlowe smiled slightly at his typewriter.

I slammed my hand down on top of the desk. Pencils bounced out of position. "Tricky Dick moved in this weekend!" I said. "Under cover of darkness, no doubt."

"I had to evacuate under a Secret Service escort," Murlowe laughed, actually looking up at me for a second. "While they secured the building."

"Richard Milhouse Nixon is our neighbor," I said, the awe in my voice more genuine than I had anticipated.

"You should have been here to protest," Murlowe said.

"Maybe it's not too late," I said. "Maybe we can go up and chant a few 'Hell No, We won't go's?'"

"You think they evacuated the building and left him alone up there?" Murlowe said. He dismissed me and returned his focus to the typewriter. "There's enough security to protect him from the entire McGovern wing of the Democratic Party."

"I think you and I, we are the entire McGovern wing of the Democratic Party," I said.

"Speak for yourself," Murlowe mumbled. "Now let me get to work, I'll give you something to keep you out of trouble."

I spent the rest of the morning underlining incomprehensible passages in circuit court cases involving air rights and power lines. The more incomprehensible the sentence, the more vigorously I underlined it. When I got bored, I sketched a power line across the top margin, a few birds silently surveying the court's logic.

At lunchtime, I took my mind off air rights by smoking a bit of hash my friend Terry had left over from the weekend. We sat in our favorite spot—the shade thrown by a new sculpture that had been hauled into Federal Square one dark summer night: Richard Serra's Tilted Arc.

"It's either an expression of the infantile revolutionary quality of bourgeois postmodernism or a radical commentary on the breakdown of the public sphere in this media driven age." I said, settling into a space on the cobblestones so that my back leaned against the wall of the Arc.

"Yeah. Or it's a 12-foot wall of rusted metal." Terry responded. "Either way it's good for lighting these matches."

He struck a blue tipped camping match against the side of the wall. "Makes me feel like Humphrey Bogart." The match crackled slightly, and Terry lifted the crooked flame to his face.

We passed the pipe back and forth in silence. I looked up at the gray of the skyline.

"I almost forgot to tell you," Terry liked to talk while he inhaled. It gave his voice a high-pitched urgency. "I got that job with Green and Lowell."

"Congratulations," I said.

"My office will be right up there," He pointed at a non-descript granite cube of a building.

I took the pipe he held out toward me, but didn't put it to my mouth. I stared at the building, which I knew was 212 Centre Street.

"That's my father's old building," I said, passing the pipe back to Terry. "He worked there for something like thirty years."

"Whoa, wait a minute," Terry said, then inhaled deeply. "Does that mean he died in that building?" he squeaked.

"No," I answered. The rusty corner of the Arc cut across the bottom of my view of the building. "That happened in the ambulance on the way to St. Vincent's."

Terry nodded, then exhaled loudly.

I listened to his breath. The haze of the air was thick enough for me to hide in now.

"I think we need to go up and introduce ourselves to Nixon," I said.

"You think?"

"Like the Welcome Wagon."

Terry tapped the pipe against the wall. It rang out like a gong, so that several of the other lunch-time art lovers standing in its shade turned to look at us.

"Sounds like Murlowe represented us."

"Greeting the fallen leader of the Free World is not a task that should be delegated." I said. "Even to Murlowe. We should take the elevator up to the eleventh floor and say hello. Make sure he has the right key to the executive washroom." I waited. Terry did not respond. I tried to say something funnier. "We could register him to vote in his new district."

"He doesn't live here," Terry said, sitting back against the wall beside me. "It's just his new office."

"Well, he lives somewhere," I closed my eyes and leaned my head against the rust. "Even Richard Nixon must live somewhere."

The warm metal of Tilted Arc pressed into my skull. I had studied Serra in college and loved him, thought he was provocative and important. Then my father died, and, in my grief, I declared pre-law. The Arc was commissioned to grace the barren plaza outside the new Federal office building, a block and a half from my father's office. I got accepted at Columbia, met Terry in Contracts 101. The finished Arc cut diagonally across the square, which had, in the meantime, become a popular lunch-time meeting spot. I had dropped out that May, Terry graduated with honors. There was a lawsuit pending to have Tilted Arc removed.

The haze glowed as if it were light itself. There were clusters of young office workers scattered here and there around our half of Federal Square, passing joints or brown paper bags back and forth, or just sharing sandwiches in the noon air. There were people hurrying to get back to their offices, and a homeless man sitting outside of an appliance box. A heavy-set man with an overstuffed briefcase came barreling diagonally toward us, his head down, his stride rapid and labored. He would have hit the steel of the Arc if I had not banged on it with the flat of my hand and called out to him, "Hey, Look up!"

He stopped and tilted his head, listening to the ringing sound of metal, then stood for a moment looking up at the wall of rust, an angry impatience developing on his face.

"What in the Holy Mother of Manna is this?" He called out, to no one in particular. He seemed not to have noticed us sitting at his feet.

"Art." I said. "Sculpture."

He looked up and down the length of the Arc, past Terry and I to his left, past the homeless man to his right. Then he looked straight up. The Tilted Arc curved around him on both sides, and leaned just enough to press down on him.

"No." he said at last. "Art is green men on horseback surrounded by untrimmed shrubbery. This is something else." He turned and circled to his right to go around the Arc. As he passed the homeless man, who had draped a quilt over one end of his box and was now sitting on a milk carton pulling stitches from a piece of cloth, he bent down and, without slowing his stride, stuck a dollar in his coffee cup.

When I got into the elevator with the bags from McDonald's, I pressed the button for 11—Nixon's floor. I was wearing jeans, a wrinkled Oxford shirt, and an old khaki blazer. I attempted to stand tall. I fixed the collar of my blazer.

The doors opened to a large lobby room decorated to look stately and official. There was a Presidential Seal woven into the carpet, and a receptionist's desk that curved to face us and took up most of the far wall. There was no receptionist, but there was a switchboard with enough buttons to connect to every department of government. None of the buttons were lit.

There were three identical doors beyond the receptionist's desk. A man in a dark suit, white shirt and dark tie, hands folded behind his back, stood not quite at attention in front of the middle door, behind the dark telephone. He seemed able to stare straight ahead without taking his eyes off me. I stepped out of the elevator and held the McDonald's bag at shoulder height. I spoke loudly and slowly, as if to a crowded room: "I would like to see the President. I have brought him lunch."

"'He does not see people without an appointment!'" I shouted to Murlowe to get above the sound of the air conditioner and to get him to look up from the book of case law he was reviewing. I squeezed the uneaten half of a Big Mac and watched the special sauce peek out the side.

"He was President of the United States." Murlowe said. "You can't just expect to have lunch with him."

"Why not?" I put an extra dab of indignation into my voice. "He's sitting in that office with nothing to do," I didn't quite believe that, but I continued. "You think Reagan calls him for advice? You think Brezhnev invites him to lunch?"

"He does have a law practice," Murlowe sighed and turned the page.

"You think a lot of people go to Dick Nixon for advice about legal matters?"

Murlowe looked up at me. "You're really getting something out of this."

I thought of that telephone full of darkened buttons, imagined a calendar open to this week, with every day empty. I looked at my own empty desk, my yellow legal pad of doodles. I realized I really did want to meet him; I really did want to bring him lunch.

"No," I lied. "I just liked the adventure. I guess I should be glad I didn't get arrested." I tapped the edge of the desk, listening to the empty drawers echo.

That was Tuesday. Wednesday, I proofread a brief for Murlowe and went home early. Thursday morning, I took the elevator to 11 again.

That giant eagle spread his wings on the rug beneath my feet, and the fluorescent bulbs buzzed above my head. The receptionist's oversized desk was still empty. The lights on the telephone were still dark.

"Hello?" I said, my voice a bit quieter than I had intended. "Anybody home? One of your fellow Americans is here…"

The door behind the receptionist's desk opened slightly and the Secret Service agent from the day before slipped into the lobby. He brushed a hand through his crew cut.

"May I help you?"

"Yes," I said, rubbing my palms down my chest to smooth my shirt front. "I'd like to see Mr.—the President."

"The President is not in."

"Really?" I was genuinely surprised. Where could he be at this hour? "Did he leave a message?"

The agent smiled slightly. "For you?"

"No, I mean saying where he was and when he would be back." The agent opened his mouth to speak, but I continued. "Are you forwarding his calls? I notice that the receptionist is not here."

"I can help you," he said. "If you have some message to leave, or some concern…"

There was a pause. I wondered what concern had driven me here.

"Could you get me an autographed picture?" I asked.

"Certainly," The agent turned toward the file cabinet against the right wall.

"I don't really want one. I want an appointment." And now it was true. It was still a prank, a college prank by an aging sophomore who just wanted to practice his best mock serious voice with a disgraced head of state, but it was also true. I did want to talk to him. I wanted to know what he did all day, how he managed to keep busy. I wanted to ask him if he had found some direction since Watergate. I wanted to see how he was getting along.

The agent stepped toward me. I stepped back, toward the elevator.

"I don't think it would be appropriate to explain the nature of my business," I said, deepening my voice and talking slowly, as if addressing a tone deaf two-year old.

As I spoke, he continued toward me, and I backed away until my shoulders touched the elevator doors.

"He really is quite busy," the man said. I flinched as he reached a finger past me and poked the button to call the elevator. I could see now that he was older than he carried himself. His crew cut hid an almost bald head, and there were deep rings of wrinkles under his eyes. Still, his neck was tightly muscled, pressing against his starched shirt collar, indicating he was probably in better shape than your average 24-year-old pothead.

"Busy doing what?" I asked. I knew the question would appear especially rude to someone dedicated to this man he was protecting, who may not have thought Watergate was really as terrible as people made it out to be. I had intended the question to be impertinent beyond the point of being rude, as if I could raise my own status by going through rude to arrogant. But I heard a genuine concern in my voice. The hard edge of political certainty was laced with genuine wonder—what do you do all day if you're Richard Nixon? The agent reached wearily into his breast pocket. I forced myself to remain still, though I thought for a moment that he was going to pull out a gun and pistol whip me. He handed me a business card.

"You will have to call for an appointment." He handed the card to me. "I wouldn't get my hopes up, but you can say you spoke to Agent Howard."

I emerged into the hot wet street and wandered over to the shade of the rusting Arc. I held the card between thumb and forefinger, as I had when I had taken it from Agent Howard. It said, simply, *Richard M. Nixon* with a phone number. The air was cool and metallic beside the arc and I looked out at the thousand people spread out before me: all races racing back from lunch; all creeds careening through the day, every class, worker, and capitalist, pushing past one another, occasionally running up against the Arc and stopping, staring up at its height, turning their heads to take in its breadth, none of them seeming to see me there, solitary and still, like part of the wall they were hustling to get around so they could get back to work.

I tried to get in to see Nixon every day for the next week. Generally, I stopped by in the morning, but on Tuesday and Friday I also went after work, and I went several times during lunch. In fact, on Wednesday I ate my lunch in the reception area. I had brought Nixon another Big Mac, and offered it to Agent Howard. He refused with a politeness that seemed simultaneously genuine and official. I ate both Big Macs and most of Nixon's fries, smiling as I thought of the story I could make out of this, though I had no one to tell the story to. I had not seen Terry in a week. He had stopped taking lunch by the Arc, had deserted our usual bars—swallowed up by the work of the law. Murlowe was there every morning when I strolled in, his face buried in some law book and he was there every evening when I left, hidden behind a page in his typewriter. When I asked if he needed help, he mumbled. I made him coffee.

It was Agent Howard I saw the most that week. The receptionist seemed to have disappeared. Though he stood at almost attention and seemed to regard me as little more than a potential assassin, he was also professionally polite and willing to answer questions, though often in single syllables.

Of course, my questions were largely facetious, slightly rude. Is he with Pat? Do ex-Presidents belong to some sort of club, or alumni association? Does LBJ ever call? Eisenhower? Does Nixon ever actually use the phrase "expletive deleted"? But as the week wore on, I began to find questions that I was generally concerned about.

"Somebody is with him, right?" I slipped a French fry into my mouth.

"Excuse me?" Agent Howard was sitting in a chair between the two doors, sorting through a pile of paperwork, making notations in the margins of blue pages he held on his lap.

"You're here, completing some sort of record keeping that I am sure is very important, but Nix—the President is somewhere else. Somebody from the Secret Service *is* guarding him. Right?"

Agent Howard let a note of tired tolerance creep into his voice. "I am not at liberty to discuss President Nixon's security arrangements." Then after a long pause he looked up at me with eyes that seem to take my concern seriously. "But yes," he said. "He is protected at all times."

"Are you jealous?" I asked.

"Excuse me?" He said, and I thought I saw him pause. He was checking the blue records against a small notebook he had just removed from his breast pocket, and I thought I saw him freeze for a split second.

"Some other agent is actually guarding the President while you're stuck here guarding his empty office. Does that bother you at all?"

He wrote a few more notes, shuffled the papers together, and put them into a file folder. He stood up, slipped the notebook back into his jacket, and crossed to a file cabinet against the left wall, and placed the folder inside a drawer. He said "No," while still facing the wall, then, having answered his last question, turned and escorted me to the elevator.

Then I arrived one morning and the office was empty. I had never seen Murlowe's chair without him in it, and noticed for the first time that he had been sitting on a white throw pillow with black trim. The file cabinet behind his chair had all four drawers open; three had been emptied.

I went to my own desk and found a pay envelope on top of my yellow pad. I heard Murlowe walk in behind me. He carried a brown file box that he placed on top of the vacant surface of his own desk.

"Moving out?" I asked.

He continued placing files from the open cabinet into the box. "They have eliminated the research staff. I'm moving into the main office." He moved a few files, then looked up, smiling slightly. "As an Associate."

"Congratulations!" I shook his hand.

"Sorry I can't take you with me," he said.

I picked up the most recent yellow pad on my desk. It had a sketch of the street scene outside the Arc, a few pedestrians in mid-stride, a sliver of skyline, some murky clouds.

"Don't be," I said.

"I didn't mean it to come as such a shock to you. I had spoken to Oakley, but I didn't think—"

I waved a hand to cut him off.

"I'm not surprised," I said. "Even Oakley had to see that you deserved it. Eventually."

"He said you could have till the end of the week to clean out your desk."

I laughed, tore the top page off that yellow pad, put it in my shirt pocket, and dropped the pad back onto the clean surface.

I would like to say that I took Agent Howard by surprise. Bolting out of the elevator at a full sprint, I hoped to get past him and into Nixon's office before even the Secret Service could react. I was not sure what I would do there—I could clearly picture throwing open the door and finding Nixon at his desk, eating a small salad or working on the crossword puzzle—but after that it was a blank. I did not have anything planned to say to him. I did not really know why I was breaking into an office protected by an armed Federal officer.

As it turns out, I did not need to know. Howard was pretty quick for a man his age. He cut off my path to the door and when I tried to get around him with a head fake, he thrust the palm of his hand into the center of my chest and I sat suddenly on the Presidential Seal, unable to breathe. I cried out hoarsely, then threw up on the eagle's left wing.

Agent Howard was very nice about it. He brought me a glass of water with another presidential seal on it.

"It's not unusual for young men to become obsessed with the President," he told me. "And not just Young Republicans. I've had to tackle members of the SDS who ran off the line on the White House tour, their hair flapping in the breeze behind them as they waved their souvenir photo book in front of them, calling for an autograph." Agent Howard was looking at some point over my shoulder, maybe at a clean spot on the rug, maybe the eagle's other wing.

"I lost my job today," I said.

Howard looked me in the eye. "You didn't seem to be such a hard worker."

"You are a shrewd judge of character."

"Part of the job," he said.

We sat on the rug in silence for a moment.

"You could tell which tourists would try to run off the line, couldn't you?"

He smiled. "Part of the job."

Agent Howard patted my shoulder and helped me to my feet. I drained the water glass and returned it to him. He held it gingerly between his thumb and forefinger, as if he might have to dust it for prints someday. I wondered if he would dust it for fingerprints later. He moved me toward the elevator, and pushed the down button.

Federal Plaza was deserted to the heat of the day. The crowds had gone off to air-conditioned offices and restaurants, or else retreated to the shade of the World Trade Center over on Chambers Street. The Arc was left alone to lean a few degrees off center. Its rust had begun to develop variations, a lighter patch where graffiti had been removed, a bit darker where the sun set's shadows had already crept onto the iron. It radiated its own challenge to the ugliness of downtown.

I crossed the square and pressed my back against it, felt as if I were melting into hot rust. I stood there staring down at my shoes. They were my father's wingtips. I had begun wearing them after I dropped out, as a kind of ironic commentary. I was not going to make law review and get recruited by a big firm. I was not going to slave for the next twenty years trying to make partner, but I was going to wear the shoes. Sometime that year, the irony drained from my father's shoes and now they were just scuffed footwear, part of my carefully constructed image of sartorial aimlessness.

The appearance of a second pair of highly polished wingtips came as a surprise, but I did not have to look up beyond the cleanly pressed cuffs on the grey wool slacks to know whom they belonged to.

"Mr. President?" I asked, surprised at my own deference. Just half an hour before I had attempted to storm his office.

"We should step out of the sun," he told me. Richard Nixon gently took my elbow and moved me as if I were fragile along the arc into the shade that had gathered at its center.

Nixon began to speak but hesitated. His nose was less prominent than I remembered it from political cartoons, but the dark shadows under his eyes lent his hesitation a completely exaggerated gravity. He reached a hand back and patted the rust of The Arc. It rang out.

"This is a serious work."

"Sir?"

"It's an important piece," he said, rubbing a hand along the rough orange surface. "Public sculpture has fallen out of favor because we can no longer express what is happening in the public square." He rapped his knuckles on the metal. The rattling throb of its echo filled the air around us. "Generals on horseback won't do anymore, but what else do we have?"

I was silent a moment. I felt unprepared to discuss post-modern sculpture with an ex-President. He repeated his question, impatiently.

"What else do we have?"

"A rusty wall?" I answered, tentatively.

"An emptied signifier. A void in the discourse." He seemed pleased, but then his voice shifted, became more ominous. "Still, it will have to come down."

"Come down? Why?"

"Because sometimes you can be right and still be wrong." He paused as if he had said something important, then began to repeat the idea, but after one word, "Sometimes," intoned with gravity and purpose, he seemed to lose interest, his voice trailing off, the final "s" floating a minute before drowning in the heat of the day. He took a breath. "Agent Howard tells me you've had a bad day?"

"Very bad, sir." My voice cracked slightly.

Nixon pursed his lips. "I am not a counselor," he said, his voice containing that familiar gravel of dishonesty, as if, perhaps, he really was a counselor. "I don't suppose you've read my book? *Seven Crises?*"

"No sir," I admitted.

"Hmm..." He reached back and touched the wall again. "But you listen to Bob Dylan?"

"Sir?"

"Carter called him a Genuine American Poet."

"Yes sir."

"Then maybe you know that he once said 'Life,'" Nixon paused now, as if this was an applause line at a State of the Union address, "'must sometimes get lonely.'"

I stood, silently, awkwardly shifting from one foot to the other.

"It would be better if you had read my book," Nixon said.

"Yes sir."

"You are going to need a job. Whatever happens today, tomorrow, you're going to need to work. Work is important. Not working is…" He stared along the wall a moment. "Hard."

"Do you have any suggestions sir?"

"Make an appointment."

He used that voice again, as if he had said something very important. "Always make an appointment." Then he rubbed his hands together as if to ward off some chill, and he left.

I remember Richard Nixon walking away from me, his shoulders hunched forward, his hands in the pockets of his dark suit pants. As I turned to leave, I noticed a bit of rust on my own hands. I rubbed them together to brush it off, stuck my hands in my pockets and slouched toward the subway.

Returns

Two weeks after Emily broke off our engagement, I found myself in the Bed Bath & Beyond on Sixth Avenue, returning a pair of champagne flutes, and hoping Emily might be returning other wedding presents. She wasn't. She wasn't returning my phone calls either, so maybe returning was another thing she wasn't doing anymore, to go along with marrying me.

The bridal section was not crowded. It was June and if you were registering for any wedding before New Year's you were already too late. I stood near the silverware patterns and watched a young blonde examine china patterns with a casual, what's-the-rush? attitude. She lifted a coffee cup to her lips, smiling as if imagining some after-dinner conversation in her perfect future, then set the cup down and pushed her cart out past the wall of cake plates.

I remembered following Emily through all three floors, examining pillowcases and spatulas, welcome mats and shower caddies. Emily had that blonde woman's same air of confident curiosity, checking off the material of our future as we walked. I remembered being bored; now I knew I should have been frightened. When I got home there was a delivery waiting with the doorman. It was a ten-piece set of anodized aluminum cookware by Calphalon delivered from Bed Bath & Beyond courtesy of Emily's cousin Marcos, the broker, who I guessed, hadn't heard. I imagined someone packing and shipping the thing while I was in the store and wondered how it had beaten me home.

I dragged the box into the bedroom, already filled with small appliances, coffee mugs, and picture frames—the world of bath and beyond gathered up like Noah's material ark, waiting for a flood. The bed, the dresser and the floor were covered—I was sleeping on the couch in the other room because I could barely enter this one, and all of it had to go back. Emily had left it all for me to keep, as if in consolation. But what was I to do with *two* 100% cotton bathrobes, or matching sterling silver frames, suitable for portraits?

The following evening, I returned the toaster oven to Bed Bath & Beyond, then dragged a patio chair over from outdoor furnishings and watched people pick out coffee makers until the store closed. Coffee makers are universal: the old and the young, single and attached, everyone compares pot sizes and brewing times. But I was drawn to the couples struggling to make a decision together: eight cups? Twelve cups? A thermal-carafe? A cone-shaped filter? They leaned together and read the boxes, or separated, calling out to each other details about timers and energy ratings.

At 8:45 there was a kind of last call announced, telling shoppers to be sure to complete purchases before closing time. That was the first time I noticed Manny moving through the aisles, resetting displays, making notes to restock merchandise. I slid the heavy metal chair with oak leaves in the armrests back to its spot at a patio table, and went home to microwave dinner.

Every time I returned something, I circled back to coffee makers, but I also spent time testing peelers and zesters, comparing shaving mirrors and examining soap dishes. I tried out a brush that only cleaned ceiling fans and used a computer program that matched the colors on sheets and bedspreads. Manny finally approached me while I was adjusting the number on a personalized mattress system.

"If you was a chick I would help you find the perfect number," he laughed.

He punched my shoulder and took my hand through a complicated set of shakes and wiggles and then threw himself down on the mattress and slapped the side, inviting me to take a seat.

"I see you here like you are some sort of inspector or something, and I figure to just avoid you. But then I seen you playing with the refrigerator magnets and I said 'He ain't no fuckin' inspector.'"

Manny worked security at night, always starting an hour before closing time to watch for shoplifters. He told me right away that he, too, liked looking at the customers. "Everybody buying things, like they must got houses big as—shit big as houses!" He laughed at his own amazement. "I'm from the projects. My moms cooked every meal with two pots, the big one and the small one." He put his hands behind his head and stared up at the ceiling. "That's why I get a kick out of watching the shopping." He sipped from the pint of Bacardi he kept in his pocket and passed it to me. "But you don't get no kind of kick. You always real serious."

We began to meet several times a week, after I had returned a set of dishes or a cordless vacuum. We would each wander around a bit, then meet just at closing time in outdoor furniture to drink Manny's Bacardi and talk about what we had seen.

"Did you catch those two men arguing over towels? I thought you were going to have to separate them."

"Skinny dude was like, 'Those are the same stripes you had when you were with Richard!'"

"Apparently the color was different."

"I can't believe skinny man bought that lie—'Oh I see now, it's more of an azure …' Kiss and make up right in the store an' shit."

"Have you noticed that people spend a lot of time picking out towels?"

"Yo, I worked at Sports Authority, and you should see white guys—no offense—white guys shopping for golf clubs. You'd think they were buyin' a second dick."

"Where do people put all this stuff?" I heard my anguish echo in the empty store. "What shelves and cabinets they must have? And then what do they do with all those Styrofoam peanuts? God, I hate those peanuts. And then you have to use it all. You have to process food and … and put pictures in the frames, and live some sort of life that someone would want to take pictures of in the first place. How do they do all that?" And I threw my arms out, knocking over a stack of plastic drinking glasses in bright summery colors, sending them bouncing down the aisle toward the citronella candles.

"Hey," Manny said. "Try not to break shit—I don't want to have to throw you out."

The Thursday I brought back the candlesticks I was examining a humidifier that could fill an 8x16 foot room with the cleansing power of steam in fifteen minutes, when Emily came running up out of the escalator hugging a queen-sized comforter cover to her chest. I ducked into kitchen utensils and grabbed a colander, holding it in front of my face to hide, watching Emily through the holes as she moved directly through the main aisle, not even slowing down at slow cookers. Last May, we had spent an hour in slow cookers.

But she was no longer browsing, just running in to pick up a comforter cover. It looked familiar—blue and gray cubes cleverly outlined in pastel green. Her Aunt Clarissa had made us a quilt with the same color scheme. That one was only partially unwrapped from its brown paper, stacked on the pile on our bed. I had left three messages asking her to come by and get it. Emily was never going to come by to get it, never going to call me to say she wasn't coming to get it. She was not going to volunteer to do half the returns, or help carry things to the post office, or have a meeting to discuss what we could keep in good conscience.

I fell into step behind her in the aisle, staying slightly to the right so I could pretend to examine olive oil-misters or hair-dryers if she turned, but she kept moving. I had to skip step double-time just to keep up with her and got a flick of muscle memory of every walk we had ever taken together— my legs floating through motions that resembled walking while her legs churned like pistons. I loved those legs and hated myself for loving them.

She zipped past clock radios, and I was jogging to catch up, still holding the colander up to block my face, when she stopped and bent low to look at a laundry basket and I bumped directly into her, lost my balance and fell forward over her back. She turned on me like I was an attacker and—pushing the comforter against my chest—shoved me back against a shelf of Tupperware. Burpable storage bins bounced from the shelves to the floor behind me. I slapped the colander onto the shelf as if that was where it belonged.

"Jeremy!" she shouted. "What are you doing here?"

"I'm returning the Salazar's candle sticks. What are you doing here?" I asked.

"I'm buying a comforter cover," she said, gesturing at the pastel bundle. She was smiling—maybe she was glad to see me? Maybe just trying to ratchet down the confrontation.

"What about Aunt Clarissa's quilt?" I asked, my voice almost cracking.

She paused and looked over her shoulder at the cash register, her desire to escape tense in her shoulders and jaw.

"Look, Jeremy. I got your messages about the gifts, about returning … dividing…." Then her eyes found mine, and that moment of fear was over. "I don't want anything. If you need help mailing things back, I can send over Caroline, but I don't want to be involved. I need a fresh start."

And my voice did crack. "A fresh start? You mean I get to keep the ice cream maker and the blender? I get both the everyday dishes and the good china? What am I supposed to do with your brother's Ray Charles obsession, or that memory of the beach at Cape May? Do I have to keep that? What am I going to do with all those towels?"

By the time Manny appeared at my side, I was screaming, but I did not want to stop. He took my elbow and tried to lead me away, saying, "Sir, I wonder if you could step over here for a moment," and then whispering "Yo, dude keep it cool, you gonna make someone call the fuckin' cops."

He tried to turn me toward the door, but I pulled away. I know that when he grabbed my arm with both hands he was trying to help, but, as I turned toward him and Emily took the chance to skitter backwards, away from me, I heard my own voice howling and I punched Manny in the face.

There are plainclothes security officers in all the big box stores. They say it's because of Black Lives Matter, but they were probably always there. For shoplifters and customers that cause a disturbance. You don't see them because they walk around pushing carts of merchandise and looking as overwhelmed as everyone else. But they see you. If you pause in front of a display of items and look over your shoulder suspiciously, if you reach into your bag, if you circle one display too often, they notice. And if you crash into your ex-fiancé screaming an incoherent diatribe about possessions, relationships, existential loneliness, then punch an employee, they're going to jump you.

I remember Manny clutching his nose, blood leaking from between his knuckles, as I was dragged to the ground. I was still shouting when they pulled me up and handcuffed me. I kicked over a row of chrome kitchen garbage cans as they dragged me from the store.

After my three days of court-mandated testing at Bellevue, and after Emily's father, in an act of unfathomable kindness, agreed to be my lawyer and secured a suspended sentence, I returned everything. I made four trips to the post office, mailing boxes to Crate and Barrel and William Sonoma and Aunt Clarissa. Then I watched the men from Restoration Hardware carry out the bed. Finally, I overloaded two shopping carts and pushed the last of the wedding gifts to that Sixth Avenue store. I wound my way through the aisles to Customer Service and found Manny had been promoted to Returns. He had a bandage that did not quite cover the split across the bridge of his nose.

I pushed the pile of gift receipts across the counter and mumbled apologies to my feet, too ashamed to look up at him. I began piling things up on the counter—the coffee grinder, the sandwich maker, the no-squeeze mop handle, all of it. Manny did not even look at me, but typed furiously into the computer and slid boxes off the counter onto the conveyor belt behind him. Each item moved through a dirty plastic curtain into oblivion. When we were almost finished, when there was only a last set of wine glasses, he spoke.

"Keep something," he said.

"No, I can't."

"You said that."

"Excuse me?"

"When my dudes Brody and Calypso was draggin' you out the store, you kept yelling back at the bitch 'Keep something! Please keep something!'"

He pushed the purple box toward me.

"I can't."

"You can." He opened the box and took out the glasses. They were hand-painted to look like blooming flowers and I knew I would never use them. Manny leaned over the counter and looked up and down the aisle to make sure we were alone, then took the Bacardi from his pocket and poured a bit of rum into each glass. He held his up in a silent toast, and then drank. I sniffed at the cloying caramel flavor –then tossed it back and put the glass down on the counter next to his. Manny put them back into the ugly purple box, and pushed it toward me.

"Have a nice day," he said. "Thank you for shopping."

A Wake

Ruth had been a sophisticated woman, one who had very little use for children. Always in suits or little dresses that seemed to restrict her movements, she existed more to be looked at than played with. Her friend Maggie was easier: round and pliable where Ruth was straight and narrow. Dressed in her soft men's suits, Maggie was a little too butch to be an aunt, but she enjoyed the role. Ruth hated being an aunt—when she came out to Lynbrook for family events, a little late and a little overdressed—there was a reluctance clinging to her like the red scarf she wore with her black dress. And she didn't like me much. I demanded too much attention, always insisting on playing the drums for everyone before dinner, making them stand around the cold basement while I practiced paradiddles and triplets. Ruth told my mother I was self-involved. I never took it personally.

Or, if I did, I forgave her when I left Bennington and moved to the city, crashing on that convertible couch in her living room. "A few nights" lasted until Ruth came to hear my band at Red Fish Blue Fish, the dark basement club where I still work. The place was cavernously empty and after the first set Ruth pointed out a job notice near the bar. She calculated the salary in bar tabs and I gave up drumming and began running the sound board for bands that actually drew listeners. I began to tell people I was into producing.

Ruth completed my shove into adulthood by advancing me the money for my first apartment.

She had a lot of friends, so it was no surprise that the funeral parlor was crowded. Maggie was playing the role of chief mourner—sitting on that tiny couch under The Last Supper, telling stories, gesturing with her cane, getting all the attention. That left me to deal with logistics and I was a little overwhelmed—talking to the manager, greeting people I barely knew. I had bought a suit and tie and shoes the week before, when we knew, and it was all a little stiff. The shoes cut a line across the bridge of my toes and my neck was on fire from the combination of shaving and a tie. I was shaking hands and hugging people and wincing up on tip-toes—craning my neck to answer the steady stream of questions—Is Evelyn here yet? Is that Rose Macher? Have you talked to Stella Simmons yet? I was already counting the minutes when I saw Jenny hesitating by the door, scanning the crowd for familiar faces before turning to sign the guest book.

Of course, it was not just her presence that made me nervous—she had loved Ruth and I had been expecting her—it was that she looked twenty-five again in that little black dress, her hands folded in front of her, clutching that tiny red purse Ruth had given her for her birthday the year before we fell apart.

The last time I had seen her she had been nine-and-a-half months pregnant with Julian… no, Madison. It had been a sun-filled day in Central Park. She was with Stillman, wearing men's overalls and an extra-large sweatshirt, both probably his, both stretched tight across her enormous belly. I remember the weary glow of sweat on her face, as if she had come in from a misty rain. She was smiling even though just standing up appeared to be a challenge and that belly and the little triangle of exposed flesh at the hip of the overalls and that perfect nose all made me slightly dizzy.

Stillman stood like his name promised, a little behind her and off to the right, one hand rubbing a spot between her shoulder blades—equal parts supportive and possessive, handsome and smug. I disliked him mostly because I thought I should, but his dislike of me seemed more specific and that struck me as unfair.

Jenny and I chatted only briefly that day—seeing her with both hands resting on her belly made me want to make excuses and keep walking before I started to cry, but she had remembered to ask how Ruth was.

"She's great," I said. "Slowing down a little."

"Ruth? Slowing?" She looked at me as if aging were my fault. "You take care of her."

I nodded.

"Tell her—"

"I will," I said, waving my way out of there.

In fact, I had been cutting through the park toward Mt. Sinai where Ruth was in for the first round of the chemotherapy no one thought would work. Maggie was refusing to leave her bedside and I had agreed to come for visiting hours to convince Maggie to go home, take a shower, get the mail or something. Give the nurses a break. I had been up late at the club and was a little hungover, impatient, anxious. I felt guilty not telling Jenny any of that, but I had an intimation that I would only discover that Stillman was not just silent but strong, able to take charge, ask all those questions I had been afraid to ask, and then call some friend at Sloan Kettering who specialized in just this sort of thing. Jenny had never tried to offer anyone's suffering anything but a little sorrow of her own and much as I craved that connection, I didn't want to deal with this new, capable partner.

Now, I maneuvered my way through the crowd to Jenny as she stood against the wall under the funeral parlor's 9/11 memorial: a picture of the wreckage, a letter from the fire station, and a scrap of American flag in a plain black frame.

"You look great," I tried to make my hug quick and platonic though the smell of her neck made it hard to conceal how much I meant it.

"You look like shit."

"Yeah, well…"

She reached out and squeezed my arm, just above the elbow—contact full of feeling, but not the feeling I wanted.

"How's Stillman?"

"Fine. He wanted to come but Madison …"

"Nice of him. To do that. Babysit, I mean."

"Ohh, they're BFFs the two of them."

"And the baby—Madison? Beautiful and charming as we'd expect?"

"Maybe more than I expected. She's kind of perfect." I could tell Jenny was trying to tone down her smile, keep her joy in check to allow for my sorrow. Neither of us mentioned that I had not met Madison and it occurred to me that, now that I no longer had chemotherapy or hospice or funeral arrangements, I would need a new excuse.

"Was it hard … at the end?"

I thought about the angry grimace on Ruth's face that whole last month, Maggie sleeping on my old couch and calling me every night to catalogue her vital signs. I remembered the way the tension in Ruth's face had suddenly eased just before she licked her lips, smiled one last time, and died.

"Only in that it was the end," I said, my voice cracking slightly.

We were silent a second, Jenny still holding my arm. She stared at the floor a little in front of her and I stared too—there was a thick carpet with ugly pink roses woven into dark blue, an expensive way to look cheap. After a moment, Jenny shook her head quickly, snapping out of some reverie.

"Where's Maggie?"

I gestured with my head, reluctant to move my arm. "Holding court over in the corner. She seems to be telling all her best Ruth stories. In chronological order."

"Well, her Ruth stories are the best Ruth stories."

"If you want, I'm sure I can squeeze you in there. She'd love to see you."

"In a minute." She looked around the room, now noticing the crowd near the coffin. "I guess I should go pay my respects."

"Ruth would wish you wouldn't."

"Why," Jenny smiled. "Is she not wearing makeup?"

"No, she is. Her instructions were very specific: closed coffin but still full makeup. She just wouldn't want to think of you kneeling at a coffin."

"Even her own?"

"Especially her own," I said. "She'd hate all this."

"She would."

A high-pitched, excited voice came to me from behind, "Josh!" And suddenly I was spun around and hugged by Bit Feldman, one of Maggie and Ruth's old friends. He took my shoulders in each hand, his grip a little shaky with age, and held me back to study me. He looked older than I remembered, his face a pasty wreck of wrinkles between incongruously dark hair and polished white teeth. "Let me look at you. You look awful."

"So, I've been told."

He turned to Jenny. "Jenny dear, you have to take care of this young man. He's suffered a terrible loss."

Jenny smiled stiffly and looked down at the floor.

"I'm okay, Bit," I said.

"No, I'm serious. I can see the strain. She needs to—oh my god," and he pulled me close again, breathlessly whispering into my ear, "I'm so sorry, I forgot you two …". Then he thrust me away from him and brushed off the front of his suit. "I must go pay my respects; I'll find you dears later."

And he stepped quickly and stiffly toward the line of people waiting to kneel at the coffin.

There was another moment of strained silence. Jenny looked down at the blurry roses. I looked at the American flag on the 9/11 memorial, at the carefully preserved stains of soot and ash.

"How are you, anyway?" she finally asked, looking up, pushing a note of casual curiosity into her voice, "I mean besides all this?"

"I'm okay. Basically."

Jenny just raised that one eyebrow that had always been her bullshit detector.

"I'm between relationships, if that's what you mean."

"Between?"

"Well, I'm optimistic anyway."

She smiled just to the edge of laughter, shaking her head and I wondered how we had gotten to this place of teasing about my sex life. I was sorry to think that I could still make her laugh even though I could no longer make her cry.

I had gone back to stay with Ruth when Jenny threw me out … asked me to leave. It was really pretty polite—more sorrow and disappointment than anger, though I guess she had run through anger on her way to sorrow. Anyway, Ruth saved me again: seven years in and I was back on that couch. It was only a few weeks this time—nineteen days—before Ruth woke up at four in the morning to find me leaning over the sink in her narrow little kitchen, my jeans scraping up against the counter on the opposite side, stuffing a Big Mac into my mouth and sipping from a forty. She told me to leave the next day—just said, "Don't be here when I get home from work," and went back to bed.

It was good though, just the prodding I needed. I found a room with two other guys on Avenue C and I was free to do late gigs at the club, hang out with the bands and the groupies. Plus, I had someplace to put my clothes and CDs and the other junk Jenny had been holding for me. I took my time getting it all, and in the end had to get a box from her the week of the wedding, which I was not invited to.

Ruth told me a little about it later. As much as I could stand. She said she and Maggie had each danced with Jenny. It sounded sweet—like they were messengers sending a blessing. I had tried to be happy for them all but mostly wished I was dancing with her myself.

We both looked over at Maggie—large and round in a black man-tailored suit, her gray hair gathered at the top of her head. She had her silver-handled cane and was gesturing with it as she told some story. Jenny made a sound in her throat, like a choked sob.

"She's going to miss Ruth."

"They were friends a long time."

Jenny turned and looked at me, a flash of anger in her eyes. "Friends?"

"Well, lovers? Whatever." Jenny shook her head, silently scolding me. "I always wondered why they never just … like … lived together."

Jenny turned away from me now—she was watching Maggie poke the rug with her cane to emphasize some point in her story. "They were scared. Then, when it was more acceptable, they were already set in their ways. Plus, rent control."

I thought about that for a moment, watching the side of Jenny's face as she spoke. The Garrisons, friends from the neighborhood, were at the door behind her, bent over the guest book. All four of them stepping up to sign, one at a time.

"How do you know that?" I asked.

She shrugged. "Ruth told me."

"She told you?"

"I asked."

I looked back at Maggie, gesturing with the cane to make room for Misty Garrison, gawky and awkward in her adolescence, coming through the crowd to give her a card.

"You asked," I said, more to myself than anyone. It struck me as an incredible piece of information. We were silent a moment, then Jenny stepped in front of me, turning away from Maggie to the line of people in front of the coffin, a giant gray metal affair with Ruth's Barnard graduation photo in a silver frame balanced on top.

"I'll miss her, too," Jenny said. "I already miss her."

"She missed you," I said. "After."

Then, in a soft, far away voice, Jenny said, "She was the one who told me to throw you out."

"Ruth?"

"After the … fights. When the tension felt permanent. One night I left work kind of dreading going home and I just went to 20th Street instead. Rang the bell and started crying when she opened the door. I was there for hours."

"Where was I?"

"I never knew where you were. I told you later I had been with Lindsey."

"Oh. That night."

"I lied. Sorry."

"I may owe Lindsey an apology."

She shook her head, slowly, as if my voice were just some background noise in the way of what she was really listening to—the hum of voices all around us, the way they formed a kind of noisy silence, the words in her head.

"I just started telling Ruth what it was like. Our marriage. Living with you. The suspicions. The lies." I could barely hear her, as if she was talking to someone else or else wanted me to lean in to listen. "Ruth never hesitated. I said you needed to grow up. She said you wouldn't."

I turned myself to follow Jenny's eyes; we were standing side by side staring at Ruth's coffin. I craned my neck around

Jordan Herbert's shoulder to make eye contact with Ruth's picture. My protector. I remembered the way she would tap her cigarette against the ashtray while she talked, always so definite, always right.

"I wondered for a while, even after I met Keith, whether I had acted too quickly." She paused, as if wondering again. "Remember you said that we should have a baby? That would help settle us?" She turned to me, a strange smile of sympathy, maybe pity on her face, as if she were remembering some silly thing I had said as a child. "I wondered about that. Wondered if you were right." She turned away again, looking around the crowd. "Then I had a baby. So now I know. *That* would not have worked."

I was having a little trouble breathing—the tie felt much tighter all of a sudden. I wanted to walk away, but Jenny was still talking in that low, dangerous tone.

"Remember the night I asked you to leave? I said—what was it—that you would go through life trying to convince people you were a member of the band?"

"Not easy to forget that night." I thought I was speaking normally but felt that same soft whisper in my mouth.

"I'm sorry I said that."

"You were angry. It happens. And maybe I deserved it, a little."

"It was Ruth's line."

"What?"

"She said it about you. The night we talked."

Jenny said something else, maybe about the baby, needing to get home. Maybe something more emotional, but her voice had faded. To tell the truth the room was spinning slightly and I was suddenly very warm, sweating a bit. Then Jenny was touching my arm in some sort of goodbye gesture and moving away. Maggie had spotted her and was waving her over, using the cane to part the crowd, let Jenny through. I couldn't bear to watch: I knew Jenny would bend down to kiss Maggie's cheek and then they would sit together on that little couch—Maggie holding Jenny's hand in both of her own.

I moved through the crowd and—cutting in front of Mrs. Munro from the laundromat—knelt in front of that gray coffin. I knew she was in there somewhere: Ruth, my favorite aunt. I pressed my hand flat against the gray metal, about where Ruth's chest, her heart might be. I pressed down, but the metal would not give. Then I made a fist and pounded on the coffin with the soft flesh at the side of my palm and listened to it bellow, a little like a drum, then did it again, and again, until I got a rhythm.

Say a Few Words

I don't often sleep with my clients.

But I remember that morning, Valerie's body curled into a fetal ball beside my outstretched figure, her bottom pressed into the soft spot in my side between my hip and my ribs. I twirled one finger through her last wisp of dry white hair then let my palm rest across the back of her bald scalp. I gazed at the knobs of her spine, which emerged each day a little more prominently. There was faint smell of medicine, and it mixed with stale perfume and Vaseline to create a calm, satisfying funk. The window was propped open by a box of tissues, and the cracked air of January was trying to push past the hiss rising from the radiator below the windowsill. I could hear the sounds of St. Marks Place below, car horns and a bicycle bell, a voice shouting out to someone named Miranda to throw down the goddamned keys. I could also hear Valerie breathing, a slow, steady wheeze, just developing into a rattle. I was smiling.

I owe my career as a eulogist to my Uncle Herbie, my mother's oldest brother, who had survived the Korean War to become the first white heroin addict in Nassau County. Herbie had an impressive talent for making money—he developed strip malls along Sunrise Highway between Valley Stream and Seaford. He also had an impressive talent for staying alive and was already over forty, having injected several fortunes into the open sore behind his right knee by the time I went to live with him. I was fourteen and, taking after my father, had run away from home. Dad was in Florida with Aunt Rachel, and Mother had become a towering goddess of propriety, incapable of fixing an Instant Breakfast without lecturing on the dangers of promiscuity and moral drift. Promiscuity and moral drift were two things I was anxious to get involved in so I stole a bottle of Mateus Rosé from Halperin's Liquor Store and hitchhiked to Herbie's apartment in Baldwin.

Herbie's rooms were bare of all furniture except a bed, a metal folding chair, and the beautiful wooden coffee table between them. We rinsed two paper cups he found in the wastebasket and pushed the cork into the bottle with a screwdriver while I tried to find ice. There was only a package of Kraft Singles American cheese slices in the freezer, so we drank the wine warm. I actually drank most of the wine.

"I have been off the liquid depressants for some time," Herbie told me, pouring his wine into my cup. "In favor of the powders." He took a small plastic bag out of a slice in the side of the mattress and laid it on the table. We listened to an old John Coltrane record as I presented my case against living with my mother. The record had a replay function and the needle would pick itself up—producing a moment of silent anticipation—then drop back down onto "A Love Supreme." Herbie nodded his head as I spoke, but it may have been in time to the music, rather than in sympathy with me. I was still getting warmed up to the subject of Mother's fixation with my sex life when Herbie interrupted.

"You can stay as long as you like, but I don't know if you can like staying here for long." He took a glasses case out of his breast pocket and a works out of the glasses case. I watched in silence as he rolled up his sleeves, mixed the white powder in the envelope with a little of the wine, cooked it down and sucked it into the hypodermic needle. Then he rolled up his pant leg and stuck the needle into a pink and pus-filled blister in back of his knee. He winced as he squeezed the needle, speaking through gritted teeth.

"The arm is too obvious. Always avoid the obvious."

He sat back down and took a sip of my wine, shaking his head rapidly. After a moment of tense silence, I went back to complaining about Mom, and he went back to nodding his head. Around midnight he stood up again and tossed a wad of cash onto the table next to the torn and empty plastic bag.

"Order us some Chinese. I'll be back."

I didn't see him for two days.

I met Valerie after the Unger funeral. The Unger twins, pretty and popular seventeen-year-old girls, had died in a car accident. When I stood at the pulpit, Valerie's bright yellow headscarf stood out in the sea of gray and black. She was sitting just where the crowd thinned out a bit, the line where pushy relatives gave way to reluctant friends. That funeral was particularly crowded—youthful death will do that—and the front of the church was packed with family and close friends and those that want to appear to be either family or close friends. The lady with the sharp eyes and the yellow scarf seemed to be listening too intently. No tears, just a couple of nods of the head. She looked like she wanted to take notes.

I was at the top of my game. The twins had been clients of my other business—tutoring for the SAT. I had seen them the Saturday morning before the accident, a few hours before Nicole stole the tequila from Dad's liquor cabinet and Ricky wrapped Mom's car around a telephone poll on Merrick Road.

In my eulogy, which I charged double for, I listed all the things that early death had robbed them of—starting with the big tragedies, like love and marriage and careers. Then I began to work a bittersweet note into the list, mentioning the trials and difficulties they would avoid, "disappointment, loss and compromise are beyond them now." I ratcheted up the pathos by mentioning the promise of independent adult lives: "life would only expect them to grow further apart, but they will stay together now," I said. Finally, in a blatant assault on the emotional weakness of my audience, I confessed to the falseness of my list: "If it seems I have idealized their youth, their energy, their beauty or their innocence, it is because we can only remember them as they were—perfect." Mom sobbed loudly and a woman behind her actually began to applaud before she caught herself. The woman in the yellow scarf was just watching me intently.

She cornered me in the parking lot behind the church while everyone was piling into cars for the trip to the gravesite. Introduced herself as Valerie Coombs and asked me to write a eulogy for her. Lymphoma. She had six months.

Mother had convinced herself that it would be fitting if no one spoke at Herbie's funeral.

"Let him get Father Hal," she said. "He gives the same sermon every week, it will work just as well for a funeral." Mother took a long drag of a cigarette, sucking it down to the filter, then coughed, spit, and lit another. "Let him get that old senile priest that never remembers anybody's name. No one who actually knew Herbie could say anything nice." She sucked again on the cigarette.

"I'll say the eulogy," I said.

There was a tense moment of silence. Mother dropped her cigarette, sparks and ashes flying as it bounced off the coffee table and she dropped to her knees to scoop up the fire hazard and slip it back into her mouth, while rubbing the ashes out of the beige carpet.

"What could you possibly have to say, that was true? And … appropriate. And true?"

Before I could begin to formulate an answer, she had pushed herself up from the floor and stabbed her cigarette out in the cake plate she was using as an ashtray and left for the kitchen.

I had received my master's in creative writing the year before, and almost immediately my ambitions had dried up like a neglected sponge. To say something that was appropriate *and* true about Herbie suddenly seemed like the worthiest of goals.

Valerie and I met the week after the Unger funeral in a Ukrainian bar near First Avenue, a very quiet, old man's sort of place. I ordered a slivovitz. I gave her my fee; she winced.

"You didn't even know those twins very well," she said.

"Well enough. I had known them for . . . months. I had seen them every week. I didn't have to make anything up to fill the time." Though, of course, I had.

"But for that kind of money . . ." She looked around the bar, empty tables, half-filled bar stools. "I would want you to get to know me first."

I brought the brandy to my lips, but did not drink. "Maybe I should keep my mouth shut, but I'm going to tell you the truth. I don't need to get to know you. You're forty years old, I'm speaking about you for five minutes, tops. I don't need real deep knowledge to summarize forty years in five minutes. Normally I talk to the next of kin, or whoever hires me. I ask a few questions, I get some stories, I get a picture in my head, and I'm good to go. That's more than your average priest or rabbi does, and they speak about total strangers all the time. You want someone who really knows you, someone who can speak from some kind of deep knowledge? You have friends for that, you have family for that." I sipped. "But most people have friends and relatives that can't write very well, can't speak very well. At least not under that kind of stress. I don't offer any real depth, but I do offer clarity. Succinct, clear, appropriate, and true. If you can get that from somebody with deep knowledge of your life, go to them.

If you can only get one—a clear message, or a deeply felt message—and you decide to go with clear, give me a call." I stood up to leave, a little ashamed for pulling the hard sell on this woman.

"Thirty-seven," she said, signaling to the bartender for another round despite the fact that I was on my feet now.

"Excuse me?"

"You said I was forty. I'm thirty-seven. I've tried surgery, chemo, and radiation. None of it is going to work. Now I am just trying to die well. I've been thinking about the funeral. I do have people who could speak about me, friends, family. But I don't want them to have to say it. I want them hear it. That's where you come in."

I agreed to four one-hour meetings, but I would charge her for them.

The next time I looked, Herbie's refrigerator had an unopened jar of mustard and a single slice of turkey, unwrapped, dry as toast, clinging to one of the wire shelves. By the time he came back it had several meals—pancakes and syrup in a Styrofoam box, Chinese food in Tupperware, and six slices of pizza, individually wrapped in tin foil. Every time I bought takeout, I bought enough for two, certain that he would come home any minute, convinced that even Uncle Herbie could not be so rude and irresponsible as to leave me alone in his apartment with just that slice of meat. I also searched his apartment and found his spare works in a leather satchel in the bottom drawer of his dresser, which was otherwise empty.

I never glamorized Herbie's addiction. He was a real estate broker, not a rock star. He kept a stolen hypodermic needle and a bottle of rubbing alcohol in his toiletries bag, wore polyester suits and nodded out in front of the TV. But when he came home after those two days—clean and freshly trimmed from the barber across the street, he sat with me and had beef chow fun for breakfast while I cooked the eggs he had brought in with him. We both drank Diet Pepsi and he told me that he had spent most of the time he was gone just walking along Sunrise Highway, had made it all the way to Babylon before turning back.

"I visited every one of my malls," he said. "The East Islip Shoppers Paradise has a great view of the sunrise. I sat on the curb and felt it, just felt it. I helped build that thing, and there it was glowing like a piece of heaven had crash landed on Long Island."

In the movies, junkies talk when they need to fix and shut up when they are high, but Herbie was the opposite. He withdrew into himself when he felt the urge, but couldn't stop his mouth when he was high. Herbie asked me about girls and school and Mother, and interrupted all my answers with stories he told with such intensity that I didn't want to believe he was just buzzing from whatever he had taken to get over the high. I didn't care: I realized that I loved him because he was a junkie and I wasn't, and was okay with him, and I needed that kind of blind, stupid acceptance just then.

The first meeting took place in the parking lot of a bar in Baldwin. We were supposed to meet inside, but I was early and there were half a dozen motorcycles out in front and I decided to wait for her outside. Her kerchief was white this time, almost phosphorescent under the street lamps. That, and the darkness, made her face less pale. She was almost cute in a leather jacket, chinos, a bit of a swagger. She immediately took my arm and led me into the bar, which was dark, sour, and deserted. I looked around, wondering where the bikers were. Valerie ordered us beers from the chubby blonde woman behind the bar.

"So," she clinked her glass against mine. "We have begun."

"What have we begun?"

"Getting to know each other."

"I am only getting to know you. And just a little," I said, drinking. "You don't have to get to know me at all."

"I've already begun to get to know you," she smiled.

"What do you know about me?" I asked, simply because I thought she wanted me to.

"You are the type of person who would tell a dying woman that she will not get to know you."

"You make it sound so … impolite."

"Was that me?"

"Okay, I get you're put off," I said. "But try this:" I shifted into my public speaking voice, deep, but with an edge of anxiety that could be actual emotion. "'Valerie was always on the lookout to correct life's little injustices, those times when we are rude or short with each other, that may seem unimportant in the moment, but that can add up to a chunk of life misspent on unkindness, recrimination. That bumper sticker, 'Mean People Suck,' only seems simplistic until you realize that it is true. Valerie taught us that mean people do, in fact, suck, and we don't have to join them.'" I stopped, sipped my beer. "Thirty seconds of eulogy written, four-and-a-half minutes to go."

Valerie pushed her glass aside and stared straight ahead at the mirror behind the bar. I looked down at my damp coaster. We were silent for a moment.

"Sorry," I said. "You seem like a nice person, and I can write you a wonderful eulogy. I will write you a wonderful eulogy. But this is not the way I usually work."

"You actually give eulogies for people you don't even know?

"I know a bit. People talk. I get jobs word-of-mouth, so I often know *of* the person. I once gave a eulogy, all I knew was the deceased's address. I talked for six minutes about what where he lived told about his life. Just his address." I paused. I tried to find her eyes in the mirror, behind the colored bottles, near the sleek new cash register. "It was a killer eulogy, too."

"I thought you knew the Unger twins."

"Of course you did. To be fair, I knew a little. Everything I said about them was true. And I had met Marty Hoffman several times."

She rolled her eyes, and reached back behind her head to straighten the knot on her kerchief. "Have you ever given a eulogy for someone you really knew?"

I paused. This was not part of my sales pitch.

"My Uncle Herbie. Herbert Finnerman."

"What was he like?"

"A total asshole."

"Wow. Did you say that at the funeral?"

"Not in so many words." I sipped my beer and tapped the glass against the table. "I found a way to tell the truth, though. What I really thought." I leaned my head back and used my speaking voice again, as if addressing the ceiling. "'Today is not the day we start to cry for Herb Finnerman. Today is the day we can finally stop crying.' I stood before everyone that knew him and I told them that he was my favorite uncle, and that his life was a complete waste." I looked at my image in the mirror, smiling slightly at the memory. "I got him exactly as he was for me, I didn't let either the good or the bad disturb the balance. Exactly." I drank.

We sat silently for a moment.

"My life has not been a complete waste," Valerie said.

"So, then this should be easier."

She reached up to the back of her head and untied the knot of her white kerchief. There was a tuft of brownish hair on her left side, and a gentle baby fuzz, glowing slightly in the light from the window, covered the rest of her scalp. The white of her scalp shone brightly, and it seemed to make her eyes darker, solid black. The effect was startlingly erotic.

I began to visit Herb a lot. Sometimes he was there, in his apartment, sometimes not. I could let myself in using the key he kept in the cracked aluminum siding, maybe finding him nodding on the couch, maybe wait there by myself until he showed up to fix. Every once in a while, I would find him there and awake and sober. Fidgety and cranky, he would curse at me and complain about having to order food for us. He never asked me to leave, but I knew that every complaint he had about me was legitimate, that he was expressing an annoyance that had something to do with who I really was. In that way, the complaints seemed like compliments, and it was only the long silences that were uncomfortable. He read my poems, though he was not interested in reading or poetry. He would simply take the folded sheets of loose-leaf from me, mutter to himself as he read, then tell me what he liked, what he didn't like, what he didn't understand. There was no sense that he was helping me, no encouraging tone or facile advice. His comments were just comments.

I first tried to sleep with Valerie on the afternoon of our second meeting. She had called me to say that we should go to the Museum of Modern Art.

"I want to show you my favorite painting," she said.

"Which is?"

"'Starry Starry Night,' by Vincent van Gogh."

"I've seen it," I told her. "Maybe we can meet for coffee somewhere and you can just tell me why you like it?"

"You haven't seen it with me. This will give you special insight into who I am."

"'The Starry Night' is everyone's favorite painting," I said. "It doesn't tell me anything about *you*. Let's meet for coffee."

She refused to budge, but agreed that we could meet at her apartment rather than on the steps of the museum. She answered the door in a plain white sleeveless T-shirt, and green hospital pants that had "Memorial Sloan Kettering" stenciled unevenly across her left hip. She had just gotten out of the shower, and her head shone with dew. It cut my breath short to see so much skin glowing with such pale light. Perhaps hearing the slight sound of my choked desire, she leaned in and kissed the air next to my cheek.

"'Starry Starry Night' is a song about the painting, '*The Starry Night*,'" I said, slightly off balance from having leaned into the kiss and found only air.

"If you say so," she turned back toward her bedroom. "I also like Cezanne's still lifes if that makes you feel better."

"I like fruit," I said.

"I feel very close to still lifes—the phrase suits me. I want to put a sign around my neck 'Still Life With Cancer,' just to flip people out." She sat on her bed to tie her sneakers.

"You don't think being bald flips people out enough?"

"You don't seem flipped about it."

"I find it kind of sexy," I placed my palm flat against the top of her head, and thrilled that she did not pull away.

"I *am* sexier now than I ever have been," she said.

"How so," I asked, moving my hand to the nape of her neck.

"I've lost weight." She stood and slid a hand along the flat of her belly. "The fifteen pounds I could never get rid of, that just stayed right here no matter what diet I tried?" She patted her belly. "Cancer took that shit away. I am at my ideal weight, my most beautiful."

"Your peak?"

"You got it. Try to appreciate it fully and don't flinch as it all goes downhill."

I bumped into Herb outside a movie theatre with a girlfriend once. Herb was coming down and had no doubt been talking at the woman for hours. Whatever mixture of coffee and Phenobarbital he was on gave him the appearance of hyperactive sobriety. She was clearly enthralled, found him charming, believed him when he said his limp was from an old motorcycle accident. He was in a gray suit with no tie, and he needed a haircut. It was a look that I know marked him negatively as a businessman, that element of sloppy laziness that eventually showed up in his work had hung about him for years. No one in his working world seemed to know he was a junkie, but everyone saw something was not straight Kiwanis Club about him. On this night, however, the slightly disheveled look offset the suit to make him cool. The woman clung to his shoulder as he began to brag about me.

"He *is* very handsome."

"Any girl with my Maxie is a lucky girl," he said, pushing her hand toward me so that I finally reached out and we shook tentatively.

I was aware that Herbie seemed in some vague way to be pressing the woman on me, despite the difference in our ages and the fact that she was so clearly enthralled with him.

"A girl like that will never leave a man, no matter what he does," Herbie insisted the next time I saw him. He had bought some beer for me and we sat and watched the Nets play Denver until around midnight. Then, unable to sit still any longer, he threw me some cash and walked out. I ordered Italian hero sandwiches and watched the porn tapes he kept on the bookshelf. I gave myself another tour of his apartment, opening one closet to look at his seven suits, and the other to look at the wire hangers and dry cleaner plastic that showed she had moved in and moved out.

Once I acknowledged its existence, my desire for Valerie grew like a weed in my chest, tendrils reaching down my arms and filling my fingers until my hands twitched on my lap like they had a vegetable life of their own. We had our third meeting at Eisenberg's sandwich shop on 23rd Street. She wanted to try the famous tuna salad before she died, but something in the smell of the tuna made her gag—her throat had appeared slightly swollen when we met outside the Flatiron building—and she had to retreat to the bathroom. I noticed a slight limp as she maneuvered through the narrow aisle past the waitress. As her arm rose up to steady herself by grabbing the back of a red booth, I had to turn away and study the menu tacked onto the wall. Nothing but the prices had changed since 1953.

Later that night I showed up at her door. She let me in without commenting on the unannounced and uncompensated nature of my visit. I sat cross-legged opposite her on the floor, a small candle between us. She poured me tea. She had a line of medicine bottles spread before her and was taking out pills and laying them on a small tapestry at her knees.

"Some of these are prescribed by the last of my doctors, painkillers, vitamins. Others I picked up at various health food stores. This one—" She picked a small reddish pill from a large blue bottle "—contains seven herbal extracts that are supposed to boost the immune system. Which is good, because my immune system has never really recovered from the chemo."

She had the pills lined up now and was moving them in and out of the line, as if they were pieces in a sidewalk con-game. Her arms were hennaed with a pattern that included flowers and spiraled tendrils. Her hands were quick and sure. She touched each pill gently as if she could weigh its medicinal value with her skin.

The room was silent. I tried to sip my tea quietly and looked for somewhere to put my legs. I was uncomfortable. She seemed in no rush to swallow any of this medicine.

"I have been having trouble with music," she said.

"What do you mean?" I asked.

"The other day I went to put on a Ramones CD. And I couldn't listen to it. I got this idea that I should not be listening to music I already know. I have a limited time and there is a lot of music. So, I went out and bought a collection of Wagner. The Ring Cycle."

"How do you like it?"

"I can't get the CD case open. You know how those cases can be. My hands started shaking." Now she lifted her fingers to her lips and slipped a pill in, leaning against the couch and letting her head fall back, exposing her throat. Her skin had been pale and sallow in the afternoon sunlight, but was perfect now. The candle picked up a verdant olive tone, and her eyes shone darkly beneath a black satin kerchief. "I thought some music might calm me down, so I put on the Ramones."

That night, when I leaned across the candle and tried to kiss her, she was kind enough not to notice.

I picked Herbie up at the emergency room when he needed to get the sore on the back of his knee drained. While I was helping him limp to his car, he complained that he had to get up the next morning for a meeting with a construction foreman and a client to schedule a project.

"These fuckers always want to meet at 8 am. They never sleep in. Don't trust people who do not sleep in."

I lay awake on his couch that night, and I heard him slipping out of the apartment at 7:30, dragging his left leg a bit as he headed to his car.

Those weeks before the overdose were like watching weeds overrun a neglected garden. All the precarious forces he had organized into something resembling normalcy had begun to rebel against his control. His leg never healed correctly, and the mixture of heroin and painkillers turned his energy level down a notch he just didn't have. He missed appointments and lost paperwork. Clients had begun to suspect something, and work had become hard to find. Now, suddenly, Herbie was short of money and hustling for drugs in a way he had never had to. He was dirty and desperate and dealing a little to make ends meet. He got arrested for possession of marijuana with intent to sell and Mother made me wait almost forty-eight hours before putting up the money to bail him out. Leaning on my shoulder as we stepped out of the back door of the county jail, he smelled like urine and disinfectant. His hair was matted and his suit was caked with something black.

"You have $200 you can lend me." It was not a question.

"Yeah," I answered. "Mother thought bail was $2,000, but it was only $1,800."

"I know," he said, folding the bills and slipping them into the pocket of his suit jacket.

I slipped out of the apartment while he was in the shower to take the dirty suit and some other things to the dry cleaner. I stopped and bought a double order of Chinese vegetables in garlic sauce at the takeout on Grand Avenue. He was gone by the time I got back. At the coroner's office the next day he was lying on the slab dressed in his pale linen suit. His shoes were shined, sitting next to his bare feet, one big toe tagged with his identification. He had gotten a haircut and a manicure. His skin was still pink and firm, but there was no doubting that he was dead. He was just good-looking dead.

My late-night visits became a regular occurrence. I found it hard to stay away, though my flirtations went unnoticed and the heat I felt when I took her hand or arranged to brush against her in some narrow corridor was entirely my own. She never acknowledged my advances, turning her head so I kissed her cheek goodbye, stepping out of the hook of my arm with frustrating grace.

There were a lot of people in her life. I sat for hours in the café across the street watching her door, waiting for them to leave. I figured out from her stories which one was her sister Michelle and which was her friend Kate. There was a tall and handsome Cal I was jealous of until I found out he was a family friend in the priesthood. It seemed she did not need me for anything more than what she was paying me to do.

But as she lost weight and balance and mobility, she welcomed my company. The first night she needed help getting to bed I promised I would wait until she was asleep and then let myself out, knowing full well I would spend the night on the couch. After a few nights on the couch, I moved into a cot beside her bed. Not every night, but a few times I was there to help her back to sleep after a night terror. When she started getting chills, I slid under the blankets, spent the night warming her. She slept fitfully while my eyes grew accustomed to the darkness and watched her breathe. In the dawn, I studied her skeleton and touched her skin, soft as petals, fragile as dried leaves.

After Herbie's funeral, people came back to the house. Not many: friends of Mother's, a few neighbors, a girlfriend who had only recently broken up with me. The chaos of his final weeks had made him a pariah, and few of his business associates even sent flowers. We sat in the living room and sipped coffee. Mother stayed in the kitchen, drinking vodka.

Before she left, Mrs. Whitehurst pressed next to me on Mother's couch, told me how much she liked my words of comfort for Herbie and asked if I would say a few words about her mother, who had died that afternoon. I explained that I barely knew her mother, but Mrs. Whitehurst insisted she would pay me. My career began.

The day of Valerie's funeral I sat in a drug store across the street from the church, occasionally touching the knot of my tie, straightening my suit jacket. It was an old-fashioned lunch counter, littered with the small items that sell in such settings—blank CDs and breath mints, vitamins that increase your sexual potency and triple A batteries. I drank several cups of coffee and watched the activity across the street. Other customers had to reach around me to get cigarettes or pay for their shampoo, but I had a clear view of the hearse and the priest greeting guests. They all wore gray and black, though Cal had a bright green prayer shawl over his vestments that reminded me of Valerie's kerchiefs. The coffin went in first with everyone shuffling behind it, Michelle, her blonde hair tied back in a ponytail, escorting an elderly woman I thought must be their mother, a man in a dark suit comforting Kate. A few stragglers arrived late and then the steps to the church were empty.

I thought about the candles and the altar, went through the Order of the Mass and wondered what readings the family might have chosen. I tried to guess what the priest was going to say, but my mind was blank—not even the most standard of death clichés would come to me. Of course, there would be no other eulogy because I was across the street drinking coffee. I expected someone might come out looking for me, maybe just a head peeking back out through the doors, searching up and down the street in case I might be late, but it did not happen.

Fifty minutes later the same crowd came out, and I could see Valerie's mother look up at the sky, her face flushed with emotion. Michelle looked down, reached behind her head and released her hair, letting it fall to obscure her face. Men scrambled to get their cars in line behind the hearse, and there was a burst of hurried conversations to make sure that everyone had seats in the appropriate cars. Even among this activity there were a few people standing around, awkwardly social, lighting each other's cigarettes and kissing each other goodbye. I counted: eleven cars followed the hearse around the corner and off toward Sunrise Highway, and a few minutes later the steps to the church were empty again. I knew if I sat there a little longer, I might see a wedding party pull up.

I paid for my coffee, tipped generously and walked up the block to the Long Island Rail Road station to wait for my train home. I sat in the waiting room and took the typed sheets of my eulogy out of my breast pocket. It was good, maybe the best I had ever written—almost as if I'd known her. I tore it into little confetti-sized bits, dropping each one to the floor until a small pile built up at my feet. A prerecorded voice called out train destinations in a monotone that seeped from the speakers and slid down the stone walls. I imagined that any minute someone would walk in and the rush of air from the door would blow my words around the room. I waited.

Jorge's Notebook

I looked at the notebook on Provo's desk, in between the telephone he was using to call Jorge's mother and the dog-eared pile of student schedules every guidance counselor kept handy. The notebook had started as one of those old-fashioned marble jobs; I had originally noticed it back in September because I carried the same kind. That coincidence had been too generic to sustain the connection I tried to draw when I showed Jorge mine and asked about his writing.

I reached forward and took it up off the desk, the cover was black and red now that the marbling had been filled in and the binding had cracked. Jorge shifted his weight toward me and I thought he was going to reach out to snatch it back, but he kept his arms folded across his chest, holding himself tightly enough that the unzipped front of his black leather jacket closed over his plaid flannel shirt. His long black hair, normally in a ponytail, hung loose below his shoulders, the one red-dyed streak running along the left side of his face. His pockmarked complexion burned a bit darker than usual, the red undertone heightened as he leaned slightly forward and watched me.

I leaned in as well, getting as close to his face as I could without spooking him. I whispered, "Remember that piece you wrote last month, the guy and his girlfriend?"

"He punches her?" Jorge asked, smiling as if flattered that I had remembered.

"What did that guy look like?"

When Jorge hesitated, Provo's elbow jutted out from behind the desk and poked Jorge's shoulder to prod him into answering the question. Since there was only one phone, Provo had squeezed two chairs behind his desk and was trying to share the space with Asada, the dean, so they could both be on the phone with Jorge's mother at the same time. They were tall men, all legs and arms, and were having trouble fitting between the desk and the wall. When Provo poked Jorge, the kid tried to move out of reach, but then his knees bumped mine and he slid back into his original spot.

I looked into Jorge's eyes, trying to hold his attention despite being distracted by the phone call myself. "How tall was he?"

"In that story? He was tall. A skinny Black guy," Jorge allowed now, his voice dismissive, as if he got my point and was way ahead of me.

"Put it on speakerphone," Asada complained.

"Why was that important?" I asked.

"This thing doesn't have speakerphone," Provo said, tapping the unit with the palm of his hand.

"You have the twentieth-century model," Asada said. Basil Asada dressed like a teenager in jeans and a T-shirt under a black leather vest that had a thick sheaf of papers bulging out of an inner pocket. He thought the leather helped him relate better to the kids. Jimmy Provo, whose eyes seemed to open a little too wide, looked young enough to be a student despite the shapeless suit jacket and the skinny black tie that was knotted tightly against his prominent Adam's apple. As they tangled with the cord and each other in the tight space behind Provo's desk, it looked a little like wheelchair basketball.

"Why was what that character looked like important?" I repeated.

"I don't know, but you made a big damned deal about it."

"We'll just have to pass it back and forth." Asada demonstrated this by moving the receiver through the air between their faces.

"Can't we just share it?" Provo asked, and held Asada's wrist as they both pressed their ears to opposite sides of the receiver.

"So did Evaliz. Remember?" Evaliz was Jorge's girlfriend.

Jorge smiled again. "She was just glad it didn't look like me. Said if I ever wrote about a Dominican with a ponytail dissing his girl, she'd deck me her own self."

"Because it was you. Except for being tall and skinny, it was you."

Jorge shrugged. There was a scrawl of graffiti—"PitBull"—in clear, readable cursive on the wall over his left shoulder. Provo's office measured maybe ten feet square, with dull gray walls that were decorated only with a few memos tacked directly into the plasterboard and a framed photo of Provo's daughter in her soccer uniform on a corner of the desk. The only window looked out on the hallway—a small square of glass reinforced with wire mesh in the otherwise plain gray office door.

"Jorge?" I paused, hoping the question would ask itself. "Today's guy's name *is* Jorge. The student he shoots, Stevenson? Sounds like the Stevenson in our class."

"My Stevenson is white."

I could see from that reddish tone to Jorge's brown skin that he was angry—he thought this was all over nothing. The door opened, bumping the back of my chair, and Elaine Grumman, the principal, slipped in with a police officer. She was a short, severe-looking woman who habitually dressed in brightly colored pantsuits that clashed with the unnatural orange of her hair. Today's purple was no exception.

"We're talking about psych eval, not arrest," she was saying to the officer as they closed the door behind them.

"Bellevue, ma'am," the officer said. He was tall and fit, with dark and definite features, squared off black eyebrows, and a sharply cleft chin. He held a pen in his hand and clicked it open and closed reflexively. A second officer, older and heavier, with more pink in his cheeks, squeezed in around the door that, with Grumman and the first officer inside, could only open halfway. He leaned back against the door as it closed, seeming not to pay attention to the room, but studying the dials on his handheld radio, turning the thing on and off so that we heard short clips of static and feedback cut off by silence.

"Fill me in," Grumman said to me, though she looked at Jorge, who looked down at his black sneakers, smiling slightly. "We have a possible threat of violence and we're determining if it's viable?"

"That's about it," I said. I had to turn and speak over my shoulder—she was behind me and—though the three of them were huddled close together, her hip was pressed against the back of my chair. She liked to touch people as she spoke to them and now patted my shoulder as if to thank me, then turned and resumed her conversation with the officers, reaching one hand up to the younger officer's elbow. He bent down to hear her whispering so low that I could not make out a word. The older officer, pressed against the door, wiped his brow with his sleeve and returned to playing with his radio. It was a tight, airless squeeze for everyone.

Back in September, when I first noticed the notebook, Jorge had shyly opened it to the first page, revealing a tag in red and black hip-hop letters boiling over with angry angles and sharp points that morphed from alphabet to explosions at the edges of the paper. I could not make out the words with any confidence, but I thought it said FuckMetal, as in Heavy Metal meets Fuck Off. He turned the pages showing me poems and prose chunks in neat block letters of black ink with occasional words in red, moving too fast for me to read any of them. These chunks were interspersed with other graffiti-style pieces, variations on that FuckMetal tag appearing on every third or fourth page.

"We'll do a lot of writing this year," I had told him. "I hope you'll let me read some of that."

Jorge had continued to smile, looking directly into my eyes, but not saying anything. The smile was small and seemed to balance some combination of tenderness and hostility. It had made me nervous, as if there were some dare behind it, and I looked back down at the book, open to a double page-sized FuckMetal, and I had felt my confidence slipping as that black and red mark looked up at me.

"But don't let me see that tag on any desks," I'd said, surprised by my sudden tone of authority. "I'll recognize it and have no choice…" I stopped myself and looked up to see that small, quiet smile. Had it changed? Broadened a bit? Taken on some quality of victory, like he had gotten me to expose my true colors?

Now it was March and the notebook was thick with used pages that refused to lie as flat as new ones. I opened the book to the page I had marked with the yellow Post-it after reading it in class. There was a small FuckMetal tag at the top of the page, then neat black lettering standing straight up:

"Z has a Glock. That gives me three. Enough to do damage. Do damage. One in each hand and niggaz be screaming. I push one into my belt and pull the other from behind my back and everything slows down and damage and damage and damage and damage."

Jorge's eyes watched me as I read, his lips moving as if he were reading along. His face still held the anger that had flushed his cheeks and forehead as he watched his classmates file out at the bell. He had stayed that color as I escorted him down the hall and the red had turned bright and accusatory as I explained my concerns to Mr. Provo, his guidance counselor. His color had never returned to normal, and his eyes shone with emotion now as he looked at me.

The noise of the room—Provo and Asada negotiating the phone and Grumman whispering and one cop clicking his pen while the other twisted alternating waves of feedback and static out of his radio—faded into a kind of silence and my chest tightened like a fist. All my rational thoughts told me I was doing the right thing and as my finger ran over the torn section of the notebook's binding I repeated the various lines Provo and I had told ourselves when I first came in, while Jorge was waiting in the hall, his palms drumming restlessly on the wall he leaned against: this is a cry for help; in this day and age this cannot be ignored; there are rules in the post-Columbine world, protocols; this kid could be a danger to himself; we don't really have a choice. But the tension in my chest as Jorge stared at me, the rapid shaking of his leg, the way he opened and closed his fists all told me I was wrong. FuckMetal had not appeared on a single wall, not one desk, not one bathroom stall. All year, he had used the names of classmates and teachers in his poems and stories, and though much of his writing was veined with violence, pulsing with repressed anger, kids generally liked showing up in his stories. He smiled shyly and kept his voice low whenever he read aloud in class. This was teenage fiction: fantasy, not threat. An angry kid venting to his sacred notebook. I should never have brought it to Provo's attention. There should not be police in the room.

I looked down at the notebook and ran my finger down the neat handwriting till I found the passage: "'I shot him in his fucking Cornell T-shirt. "Today the ivy league runs red." I sneered.' What are you always on Stevenson's case about? What does he always wear?"

Jorge turned away, that smile creeping out like he could not help but enjoy himself.

"Say it, Jorge: he wears college T-shirts."

"Every fucking day," Jorge muttered.

"So, is this fiction?" I asked.

Jorge snapped his mouth closed—I heard his teeth click together—and just smiled. He looked at me.

Provo and Asada had finished practicing and had gotten Mrs. Valencia on the phone. They were trading the receiver back and forth with Provo speaking to Mrs. Valencia in English and then passing the phone for Asada to translate, each leaning in to try to hear what was being said whenever the other had the receiver, leaning away to get some privacy whenever they had it themselves. Mrs. Valencia spoke loud enough—in Spanish with occasional English words—for all of us to hear her comments and questions.

"It's not a threat or a plan, is it?" I whispered.

He simply held my gaze in that slightly scary way he had.

"I get that you're mad at me for starting this, but now we need to convince these people"—I gestured to the room—"that this is fiction. If they think this is true, they'll lock you up. Take you to Bellevue."

His eyes shot at me, his cheeks puffing as he sucked in air, accentuating the clusters of acne scars. He bit his lower lip. "That's what they said?"

I nodded.

Jorge turned away again. He seemed to speak to the wall, "So tell them it's creative writing." He stretched out the last two words in a kind of Ferris Bueller imitation of a white voice.

"It can't just be me," I pleaded. I put my hand flat on the notebook like it was the Bible at a swearing-in ceremony. "You need to tell them."

"You tell them." He didn't look at me, but twisted his face as if angry at the wall. "You tell them what's creative writing. You tell them what's 'use your imagination'."

"You write a character who looks like you, with your name, who kills another student and then goes home to the Bronx—where you live—and kills his mother." I pleaded. "You need to be the one. To convince them."

"No," he looked at me a moment, his face tight, his eyes shining, then he turned away again. "I don't."

Grumman leaned forward and whispered theatrically into my ear. Her head was too large and square for her small, soft frame. Her orange hair was sprayed into a stiff helmet. Her face was deeply lined with a concern I could not hear in her voice.

"What's Mom like?" she asked.

"She came to Open-School night," I answered. "Asada translated for me. She wrote down everything I said." I remembered her round face and the cheap, clean overcoat she wore against the November chill, the way she scribbled notes in the margins of Jorge's report card, which was all Fs except for a B+ in English—like Holden Caulfield's I told her. She did not smile at that, or at anything else I said.

"You get along with Mom?" Grumman asked Jorge, who stared at her silently a moment before he turned away.

"Based on other things he has written," I told her, "there are some issues there."

"What kinds of issues?" she asked, her voice efficient and concerned. I needed to search for words to formulate an answer and she changed the question before I found any. "Bad enough to want to kill her?" She seemed to ask me but watched Jorge stare at the wall.

I knew I would never find the words to answer that, couldn't really believe that she wanted an answer, so I said nothing.

"She dies in today's writing?" Grumman asked.

"At the end. After killing Stevenson—the character in the class—he—the protagonist—

takes the subway home and shoots her."

"He'd never get that far," Grumman said. She stood as tall as she could, glaring at Jorge, placed her hands on her hips and tried to toss her bright hair, too stiff to really move, before turning to the officers. "Would he?"

The officer who had been clicking his pen open and closed pushed himself away from the wall and stood up straight for a moment. The fist that held the pen jutted out in front of his blue chest. "It would be our goal to prevent that, yes ma'am." He remained standing, turned toward Jorge, shifting his feet slightly to square his shoulders with the boy's face. "If Principal Grumman perceived a credible threat…" he clicked the pen. "Where you might pose a danger to yourself or," he clicked the pen "to others," click, "we would take you into custody and deliver you for a psychiatric evaluation."

Jorge was staring at the officer, the only sign of nervousness the flashing skin visible in the tear of his black jeans as his knee bounced up and down.

"Just an evaluation?" I asked. I watched Jorge who was still staring at the officer, his leg working like a piston.

"Until they are satisfied that the subject is not a danger," the officer said, not turning toward me. "At that point, if the subject has already engaged in violent or criminal behavior, we would continue to hold him."

The second officer made a show of looking at his watch and interrupted, looking at me, "If he hasn't done anything, the evaluation takes a few hours, but if they get a late start, they hold him overnight."

The first officer held his gaze on Jorge. "They can hold a subject for a two-week observation and evaluation. Without a court order."

We were all looking at Jorge now. His face was red again and he stared back at the officer, his lips moving as if he was talking to himself, but I could only hear the pull and push of his breathing. The officer with the pen looked casually down at his feet and rubbed the toe of one patent leather shoe against the back of his calf to buff a spot, then held the toe forward to watch it shine in the fluorescent office light.

Jorge unfolded his arms from in front of his chest. His right hand came up and twirled a silver stud on the collar of his jacket; he zipped the jacket closed. I thought he was going to speak, but his lips simply moved silently as if forming words on a frequency none of us could hear. Then his arms refolded themselves against his chest, stiffer and higher this time.

"So," Grumman stepped forward, "we have a threat." She looked down at my lap as if addressing the notebook. "A piece of writing that seems to indicate you are a threat to others and yourself." She turned to Jorge, "Is that threat credible, young man?"

Jorge turned away quickly, his head snapping to the side as if he had been slapped. The smile was tighter now, more forced. It seemed more like makeup—something applied to his face rather than bubbling up from inside. He sat silently staring at the wall. Behind him, Provo and Asada were still talking to Mrs. Valencia.

"Talk to him," Provo said. "Would you like to talk to him? *Por favor?*"

He reached the receiver across Asada's chest, the cord tangling in the various piles of paper on top of the desk, then he used his other hand to pick up the base and move it to follow the receiver. He had to tap Jorge on the back, the dirty white phone against the black leather of Jorge's jacket, to get his attention.

"Talk to Mom," Provo said. But Jorge simply turned to look at the phone, then turned back to the wall. Asada put a hand on Jorge's shoulder and gently spun him toward the phone.

"*Es su madre!*" he said, as if shocked at this behavior. Jorge sighed and took the receiver. I could hear his mother's rapid-fire Spanish even before Jorge pressed the phone to his ear, tight, as if to prevent us from listening in, and slowly bent forward in his seat until his face, the phone, even the hand that held the phone were only inches above his knees, hidden behind his long black hair, that one red streak hanging from his temple down past his cheek to where it met the torn knee of his jeans, still shaking nervously. The bending over and hiding behind his hair might have obscured his voice if Jorge had said anything, but he didn't.

"Is she going to be helpful?" Grumman asked Provo.

"She's going to try," Provo said. "She is concerned about him, but frankly," Provo paused while copying notes into the spiral casebook he kept by the phone. "There are issues."

"What kinds of issues?" Grumman sighed.

Provo raised an eyebrow as if to say that it was a stupid question.

"*No, Mami,*" Jorge said, his face still covered by his hair as he stared at his knees. "*No.*"

The adults in the room—two police officers, a principal, a guidance counselor, a dean of discipline and an English teacher—all listened to this boy now, his black leather jacket zipped tight, the one knee jutting out of his torn jeans wiggling furiously, his face hidden by his hair. We had him surrounded in this tiny, windowless office, his chair backed into the corner as we heard him argue with his mother.

"No," he said again, his voice sounding like English now, full and clear, wavering slightly with suppressed emotion, then, after another pause, the Spanish inflection returned: "*Mami, no!*" and his hand shot out, bringing the phone from behind his curtain of hair, and he leaned out of his chair, past Dean Asada's arm and hung up the phone. He sat back in his chair and threw his head back forcefully, swinging his hair up so that it streaked along the wall behind him like a paintbrush that left no mark before falling into place behind his shoulders. He faced up toward the ceiling with his eyes tightly shut for a moment, then resumed looking back at us, his eyes glistening in the fluorescent light.

After a moment, Grumman asked, "What did Mom say?"

But Jorge only forced himself to smile.

Now the officer with the radio handed it off to his partner and slipped into a crouch close in front of Jorge, his hands on the arms of Jorge's chair—two chrome tubes curving toward the back of the chair, one with a slab of blond wood as an armrest, the other with two holes for the screws that had once held an armrest. Jorge hugged his own arms closer to his chest, the tension in his body competing with the smile on his face, the two attitudes fighting for dominance: frightened and lonely versus independent, even slightly amused.

"Okay, Jorge," the officer said, pronouncing his name Horr-rr-HAY, slowly, in an accent even more perfect than Asada's. "It's time to make a decision. Do we want to go to Bellevue, or do we want to go to class?"

Jorge's smile got brighter. "I get to choose?"

"Nooo," the officer shook his head slowly, smiling at Jorge's smile. "Your principal, Ms. Grumman, gets to choose." He jerked his head backwards to indicate Grumman, who stood behind the crouched officer, her own arms folded in front of her chest, pulling the jacket of her pantsuit closed, leaning up on her toes, still barely taller than Jorge, who was sitting down. "But you and me get to give her advice." He counted off on his fingers, "You don't have a weapon. You have no history of violence—right?" he looked over at Asada.

"That's a twenty," Asada said.

"You don't seem violent or out of control."

"Thank you," Jorge said, as if this was a point he had been making for some time that was finally being conceded.

"But," the officer held a finger up to signal to Jorge that he was changing directions. "You wrote that you wanted to kill several people, including your own mother. You showed that writing to someone," Jorge glared at me for a moment then returned to looking at the officer's shoulder, "and even though all you have to do is tell us you didn't mean it, tell me now you are not going to hurt anyone, you won't say a word."

Jorge opened his mouth as if to speak, but the phone rang and he bit his lip and turned his head toward the wall. The officer shifted his weight. I heard his knee crack as Provo answered.

"It's Mom," he said to Grumman.

I leaned over the officer's shoulder to get as close to Jorge's face as I could, then whispered, as if somehow that granted us privacy, "If you don't speak up, we're not going to have any choice." I tried to sound rational, but heard the anger rattling in my throat. "It won't be my responsibility."

Jorge's smile unfroze for a moment, broadened mockingly. "No?" he asked.

"Let me talk to her," Grumman said, reaching for the phone. "Mrs.," she turned the paper on top of Provo's desk to face her, "Mrs. Valencia, this is Elaine Grumman, the principal. *Si, el principal.*" I could hear a voice on the other end, but Grumman cut her off.

"You understand what your son has written? *Comprenda escrita?* Yes, he said he would kill people. Here." She paused. "Yes, he said he would kill you. Mrs. Valencia, I need to know if it's true. *Verdad?*" Grumman paused, moving the phone from one ear to the other, removing an earring from the first ear with her free hand, and moving the phone back. "I'm sure he's not a liar, *no metiroso,* that's not what I'm asking. I'm asking if he's violent. Dangerous. *Peligrosso?* Would he hurt people? Put himself in danger?" Pause. "It undoubtedly would be a sin, Mrs. Valencia, but that's not—I can't wait for him to go back to church," then she took the phone away from her ear and we heard Jorge's mother say, in heavily accented English, "He's a bad boy. Dangerous. *En peligro.* Help him, please. *Por favor!*"

I noticed that she said, "In danger," rather than "dangerous," but no one else cared about the distinction. At the word "*peligro*," the crouching officer stood up and took his radio back from the officer with the pen. He was turning the radio on as he opened the office door a crack and squeezed out into the hallway.

"Thank you, Ms. Valencia. I'm going to give the phone back to Mr. Provo. He'll tell you about the hospital Jorge is going to. Yes, *hospital*," Grumman pronounced the word "hospital" with the "h" almost silent, as if she spoke Spanish.

Jorge stiffened. His arms peeled slowly away from his chest and came down on the armrests where the officer's had been. He gripped the chrome bars tightly.

"Elaine," I asked. "Can we talk about this outside?"

Her voice had a clipped efficiency, looking down at her feet a moment, she touched my arm. "All we're going to talk about is how bad we feel." She squeezed my arm for a moment and then turned to the officer with the pen, who was now writing in his black pad. "Officer Captree, I need this young man removed from the building. I am asking that he be taken for a psychological evaluation."

"Jorge," the officer said, finishing his writing and putting the black pad into his large back pocket. "I need you to stand up now."

Jorge jerked to his feet, almost as if standing at attention, his face frightened, the smile more like a wound than an expression.

The officer handed a printed card to Provo. "This is the address and phone number to give Mom. It's after one, so he'll most likely be held overnight, but she can call and find out directly from the switchboard."

I slipped into the hall, still holding Jorge's black and red notebook. For once the halls were quiet, except for that first officer, who had moved down toward the elevator and was speaking into his crackling radio. He leaned against the wall to the right of the elevator's industrial gray doors, tapping one foot in a steady rhythm while he spoke into the handset. There were a few minutes left in seventh period; students would begin leaking into the halls now before the flood that came when the bell rang. I wondered how they would react. I heard myself saying that I had no choice, that it was for Jorge's own good. I did not sound convincing.

As if he had radar and knew my patience was thin, Franklin came out of the boy's bathroom with the long loose stride that always seemed closer to dance than transportation. He was tossing one of the large plastic bathroom passes into the air with his left hand and catching it with his right when he saw me and did an instant 180-degree turn heading back down in the opposite direction, but I called out to him.

"Franklin!"

He turned and looked at me, his smile exaggerated but polite.

"Do you know Jorge Valencia's girlfriend? Evaliz?"

The smile turned bright and genuine. "You know I know her. I know all the girls."

"Where is she now?"

Franklin looked around, as if she might appear in the hallway with him, as if this was a quiz question he did not know he was supposed to study for.

"I mean what does she have seventh period?"

"Math?" Franklin guessed, smiling. "Lunch?"

"Find her for me. Bring her here now."

Franklin took a step back and forced the smile from his face. "You gonna write me a pass?"

"Don't bother," Provo said, behind me. He was coming out of the office, first in a line with Asada and Grumman, then Jorge and the final officer behind him. "She's not going to wait." He jerked his head straight back toward Grumman. He turned to Franklin. "Go to class," then quietly to me. "The decision is made." He was putting on his coat.

The group moved past me toward the elevator.

"Mr. Provo," Grumman said. "You're with this young man till Mom gets there. I want you to call me no later than 4 pm with an update."

"I spoke to my babysitter," he said, zipping up his brown leather bomber jacket. "I can stay until we know something."

"Don't kill yourself," Grumman said. "You're back here at eight tomorrow. Just stay till Mom arrives."

We were moving slowly as a group toward the elevator, Jorge held himself stiffly, as if too-consciously trying to look relaxed.

"Mr. Logan," Grumman said to me. "Do you have a class now?"

"AP American Lit," I said. "Eighth period."

"Come down and see me when you are done. You'll have to write this up."

The elevator arrived, its doors giving their high-pitched whir as they lurched open.

"Jorge," I said, a bit too loud, my voice unsteady. I reached out to hand him the notebook I was still carrying, the black of the cover fading in the limp hallway light to a wash of gray. He took it and slipped it high up into the armpit of his leather jacket without looking at me. Then, as the elevator doors closed on the group, Asada, Grumman and Provo, Jorge with an officer on either side, all of them turning to face the doors and me standing in the hall, Jorge looked into my eyes, a hard, dry stare, that surreptitious smile gone now, his face blank and brown as his eyes lost all emotion. Without shifting, they looked beyond me as the elevator closed and I found myself staring at the gray doors.

The Assistant

Crouched in the bottom of the disappearing phone booth, listening to Mr. Stamp tell the audience that the silver rings he was banging together were perfectly solid, Raquel could smell the stale sweat and deodorant in the fabric of her leotard. There was a spot of rusty brown on the knee pressed close to her face—blood from the slice the trap door had cut in her thumb in Sloatsburg two nights earlier, at the junior high. She still wore a Band-Aid, but knew she could not put off the laundry another night.

Mr. Stamp had bandaged the cut and given her aspirin after the show.

"Salicylic acid enhances blood flow," he'd said in the same serious, matter-of-fact tone he used when registering for motel rooms or explaining trinomials.

She had lifted the bloody toilet paper away from the slice in the pink ball of her thumb. "I'm not sure blood flow is the problem," she said, smiling in a way she hoped looked witty.

Mr. Stamp had put the Band-Aid on very tight—this was in the front seat of his station wagon, its faux wood sides barely visible in the dark lot behind Kill Van Kull Junior High School, all the props and equipment stashed in the back. Mr. Stamp was still in his tuxedo, Raquel in the pale blue leotard with pink beads sewn along the neckline, the little offset navy-blue skirt hitched up under her on the bench seat. He let his own large thumb press down on the plastic of the Band-Aid until Raquel winced slightly, his voice tense with patience. "Nothing happens if the blood doesn't flow," he'd said, and he took the tissue from her hand and stuffed it into the litter bag hanging from the cigarette lighter. Mr. Stamp did not smoke. Then he turned back behind the steering wheel and asked her to fasten her seatbelt. "That's why we're careful," he said.

At the hotel, before disappearing into his room, he had gestured at her door as if he could see behind it. "Phone home tonight," he'd said. "Tell your mother about the injury. I promised: no surprises."

That had been in Sloatsburg. Tonight, they were in Paramus and she had to get back to washing his shirts and her leotard. For two nights he had only insisted that she reload the trick bouquets, taking care not to tangle the petals in the spring loader as she pushed the silk flowers firmly back into their tubes. She had kept the sound low on the TV bolted to the dresser in her room so he wouldn't know she was watching and come in to make that speech about distractions and a job well done. She wondered what he did in his room. Whenever she went to say good night, knocking on his adjoining door and then standing in the passageway between their rooms, he had his itinerary binder with all the shows and hotels for the whole tour sitting on his lap.

When Mr. Stamp and his wife had first moved around the corner from Raquel on Tuthill Road, everyone knew they were planning on having children. They brought it up at cookouts and when the mothers got together on the sidewalk they included Mrs. Stamp. But, after a long time, Raquel noticed the mothers shaking their heads whenever Mrs. Stamp went back to her kitchen. "What a shame," her mother whispered to Raquel's father, and told Raquel to always be nice to Mrs. Stamp. "Let her give cookies to the twins. Make sure they say thank you." But when Mrs. Stamp came out with a tray, the cookies turned out to be the healthy kind—sugar-free with carob chips instead of chocolate—and Raquel had to hide the half-eaten remnants in the pocket of her jean jacket.

Mr. Stamp walked to work at the high school every morning during the school year, carrying a briefcase and striding stiffly, as if someone were watching. Once Raquel's father, at a parent-teacher conference, joked about being jealous of his commute, but then said to Raquel's mother on the way home that he would rather ride the Long Island Rail Road a thousand miles than be stuck in a classroom with all those shitty teenagers.

Mr. Stamp was a good teacher, clear and well-organized. The other girls crushed on Mr. Freeman with his blond hair and the quaver in his voice as he read *Our Town* aloud in class, but Raquel was a math girl and she thought Mr. Stamp's explanations of oblique triangles and cosine functions could be invitations to a world of beauty and enchantment.

When Raquel's mother sent her around the corner for extra help before the Regents exam—Better safe than sorry, she'd said—Raquel had seen that Mr. Stamp's study was divided in two. One side was math, with a row of textbooks along the back of the desk and a poster of Albert Einstein above the filing cabinet, while the other side was magic, an image of Houdini partly blocked by the disappearing phone booth. While Mr. Stamp explained the derivation of polar coordinates, Raquel kept looking over at the magic side, at the props and equipment, at the flyers with his stage name—*Dr. Wonder!*—advertising old shows in places like Pittsfield and Hartford. His tuxedo hung from a hook on the wall next to the sequined leotard Mrs. Stamp wore as his assistant; the hangers in their shoulders held the clothing stiff and still, suspended over an old suitcase. When Mr. Stamp was satisfied with her trigonometry, he showed her how the disappearing phone booth worked, letting her fold herself into the hidden compartment and smiling as Raquel imagined a spotlight and made a special effort to unfold gracefully before taking a bow.

A week before Raquel was to graduate, Mrs. Stamp tripped over the shovel while planting zucchini, and broke her ankle. She used crutches to come all the way around the corner with Mr. Stamp to meet with Raquel's parents. They sent Raquel to the basement to watch the twins while they discussed whether she could be Mr. Stamp's assistant that summer.

The basement was always a little cooler than the rest of the world, and, after the spring rain, it felt damp and clammy. The twins were at the bottom of the stairs, spread out on the yellow shag remnant that covered the patch of the cement floor Mom had denoted the play area—across from the washer-dryer. A game board was spread out between them, a third pile of money Raquel was ignoring spilled out from one edge.

"All expenses paid, of course," Mr. Stamp had said. "Motel rooms, meals, everything."

"And five dollars a show?" her father asked. Mr. Stamp nodded. "That's good money."

"Hotels?" her mother said. "Hartford? Rensselaer? She's only seventeen."

Raquel was at the top of the basement stairs, leaning into the crack in the door she held open, one hand on the doorknob and one flat on the wooden surface next to her ear, her face pressed into the opening. She strained to hear what they were saying, to understand what direction the conversation was taking.

"You know where I was at seventeen?" her father asked.

"It's different," her mother whined. "For a girl."

"We were in Kaesong, Pusan. Korea, right Stamp?" He slapped Mr. Stamp on the shoulder.

"Well, I was nineteen. Draft age," Mr. Stamp said, and even Raquel could hear that he was put off by her father's boyishness. "But yes, I get your point."

Raquel thought of seeing new places, checking into fancy hotels, ordering room service. She imagined Mr. Stamp, handsome in his tuxedo and, remembering Mrs. Stamp's beautiful leotard back in the office, imagined something even more beautiful for herself—baby blue, maybe rhinestones. This was adulthood, she thought, as she listened to Mr. Stamp's voice explaining how stage work taught poise and responsibility. She wished that he was more persuasive, exciting, wished he sounded more like magic, less like math.

Mrs. Stamp leaned forward and put a hand over Raquel's mother's hand. "I know what you're thinking," she said. "My husband is a good man. There's no cause for worry."

When her father called her into the room, there was a moment of silence after his booming voice as Raquel, pausing to get her happiness under control, took a deep breath, ran her hands down to smooth the skirt over her hips, then pushed through the door to join the grownups.

Mr. Stamp did a tour of the tri-state area every summer, magic being his serious hobby. Starting in Port Jeff, where they lived, they crossed on the ferry to Bridgeport and did their first show at the junior high school, then went on to a PTA benefit in Waterbury and the Granby Senior Center. Then Millerton, Coxsackie, Herkimer, almost as far as Syracuse before turning back toward home. Some days they did two shows—VFW and Knights of Columbus, birthday parties, that one legit theater on Olde Vaudeville Night in Ellenville. By August, it was all familiar to Raquel. They had turned around after the Oneida Volunteer Fire Department and now every stop brought them a little closer to home.

The lighting at the Rocky Marciano Sons of Italy Lodge in Paramus was spotty and Raquel knocked over the magic rings when she spun into the disappearing phone booth—a plywood crate painted red to look like it was from London. Spinning and letting the little skirt around her hips flare out to show her legs had been her idea, and she knew Mr. Stamp only put up with it reluctantly. As the rings rattled around on the floor of the little stage, the three boys in the back row laughed and slapped each other's hands. Raquel stiffened her smile and waited for Mr. Stamp to close the door.

It was pitch dark in the booth. Raquel let her fingertips graze along the wooden sides as she folded herself into the crouch and pulled the lid down over her head, careful to keep her thumb out of the way this time. She slid the false front into place so that, when the door was opened, it would look like she was gone. There were slats for air but she began to sweat and noticed the smell of herself and the dirty leotard. She rubbed a finger over the Band-Aid. There was a thin slice of light above the hinge and through that tiny crack she could see Mr. Stamp moving about the stage, gathering the fallen rings and doing the patter that accompanied turning them into a chain, a trick that usually came after the disappearing phone booth. That meant Mr. Stamp would keep her in that tight, silent crouch a little longer than usual, but it was her own fault. She could hear those boys hooting at the trick.

Back in June, Raquel had thought she would like being on stage, but the truth was she simply handed Mr. Stamp his props and posed in silly positions that signaled the audience should applaud. Mr. Stamp had let her design her own leotard and she had used her mother's old Singer to sew on all the spangles. She knew she was prettier than Mrs. Stamp, who had stiff, straw hair, but Mr. Stamp paid little attention to her and it unnerved her. She noticed some men in the audience watching her when they should have been watching Mr. Stamp pull an endless rope of handkerchiefs from some woman's purse.

She especially disliked it when there were teenagers in the audience. These three boys, slouching in the back, the one curly-haired kid with his legs draped over the chair in front of him, laughing at every trick and calling out theories of how they were faked—"It's up his sleeve," he yelled when Mr. Stamp made the woman's bracelet disappear. Raquel fought the urge to stick her tongue out when Mr. Stamp pushed up his sleeves and found the bracelet on the husband's wrist.

The movement of the door as Mr. Stamp opened it the first time to show she was not there pushed a gust of hot air down into the hidden compartment and she heard that curly-haired boy call out, his voice a sarcastic sneer, "Oh no! Where'd she go?" Raquel pressed her face closer to the crack of light, searching for cooler air and a view of that boy, his sloppy hair and Twisted Sister T-shirt. She wished there was a trick that would win them over, that Mr. Stamp could rise to the challenge of their heckling, but when he finally opened the door and she stepped out, her arms wide despite the dark rings of sweat under her armpits, a practiced surprise on her face, one of the boys whistled. She did a graceful half turn so that her torso was between Mr. Stamp and the middle finger she stuck up at the back row.

When Mr. Stamp and Raquel came out to the parking lot, each of them carrying one end of the phone booth and a bag of other props over one shoulder, one of the boys was waiting for them. He stepped out from between two cars, and Raquel started slightly, causing the canvas bag to slide off her shoulder and down her arm to where her hand was lugging the booth. It was not the curly-haired boy, but the quieter one with the hint of mustache who had sat next to him, laughed at his jokes.

"I liked your show, Dr. Wonder," he said, using the stage name without irony. He looked at Raquel as he spoke. He was not cute—skinny with no chin—but he had nice eyes. His voice was polite now, maybe a little eager. "Can I help you with that?"

Raquel was wrestling a little bit with her end, holding the booth with one hand, raising the other above her head until the straps of the canvas bag slid back down her arm, shrugging them onto her shoulders and grabbing the booth with both hands again. The boy took a step closer to help, but Mr. Stamp made a noise in his throat, something between a cough and a word, and the boy stopped. Mr. Stamp rested his end of the booth on the bumper of the station wagon and nodded at Raquel as he fetched the car keys from his pocket. She lowered her end to the pavement, same as every night, and hurried to take the keys from Mr. Stamp, who raised that end of the wooden booth high enough for her to lower the tailgate. Mr. Stamp rested his end of the booth on the tailgate and both of them went to the back end to shove the length of the crate into the wagon.

The boy stood watching, a tuft of brown hair covering one eye. Mr. Stamp brushed his two hands together as if they were dusty.

"You'd better get home now, son," he said.

The boy looked at Raquel once more, then turned and left. Raquel watched the boy walk away, shoulders stooped, hands in the pockets of his Members Only jacket, while Mr. Stamp closed the tailgate. On the drive to the motel, a Holiday Inn outside Parsippany, the two were silent until Mr. Stamp parked and, just before going into the office, said, "We have to be careful about knocking things over on these small stages. Maybe cut the twirling."

The desk clerk, some girl around Raquel's age, or maybe twenty, with stringy hair and a Huckapoo shirt with the New York City skyline tight across her chest and stomach, was studying from a giant economics textbook that she had to move so Mr. Stamp could sign the register. Desk clerks usually stared at them when they signed in, even though Mr. Stamp made a show of getting two rooms and always referred to her as Miss Adelman, his assistant, and made her carry her own luggage. This girl barely looked up from her book. Raquel shook her head slightly because, after all, she was checking in to a motel with an older man in a tuxedo. And she was wearing a leotard. Mr. Stamp turned away from the desk and handed her a key and repeated the room numbers, 216 and 218, before going back out to find the staircase. Raquel paused a moment, thinking this girl would look up and smirk, or say something, or even just notice she was there, but the girl stayed focused on her textbook and, after a beat, Raquel followed Mr. Stamp out.

They had gotten Burger King take-out for dinner because it was her turn to pick, and she ate her Whopper and fries in front of the TV. This one was bolted to the desk, the faces on *Hollywood Squares* all a little too green. As she was finishing the shake, she heard Mr. Stamp knocking on the adjoining door.

Raquel jumped up and crossed to open her side, wishing she had turned the TV off, that she had been watching *Nova* or the news. She stood in front of him. She was still in her leotard. He had removed his shirt and tie, wore just the black tuxedo slacks and a white T-shirt. He seemed, as usual, to avoid looking at her, his eyes on perhaps her hairline, or a spot on the wall behind her. "Excellent balance during the levitation tonight," he said. "You stayed perfectly still." Raquel knew he was making up for criticizing the twirling, but she smiled and said she liked levitating best and there was an awkward silence, the two of them standing on either side of the adjoining doors, until finally he coughed and said, "That boy? In the parking lot?" Raquel nodded, afraid to say anything. After a moment, Mr. Stamp said, "I know his type," and handed her his two tuxedo shirts—the one he had worn that night and the one she had not washed after Sloatsburg. Then he stepped backward into his room and closed the adjoining door on his side. Raquel heard him turn the lock.

His voice, she thought, was always so clear and, she searched for a word from the SAT lists she had studied. Forthright? He always sounded like he was teaching, even when he was on stage. He was good at the tricks, Raquel understood, but not very entertaining. And yet, that patient, direct description of what he wanted the audience to believe seemed to fit the rooms they appeared in, with their fluorescent lights and institutional colors.

She let the sink fill with hot water and sprinkled soap flakes over the surface. She pushed each shirt, one at a time, into the soapy water, pressing the bubbles of fabric that floated to the top, squeezing out the air trapped underneath. She drained the sink and refilled it twice again, rinsing the shirts with water as hot as she could stand it, then wringing them out and putting them on their wire hangers suspended from the shower curtain rod. She thought of what her mother always said, a cigarette hanging from her mouth—Thank God for permanent press.

Later, after she had washed the leotard, hung it up to dry beside the two shirts and taken her shower, Raquel sat on the bed in her pajamas with *The Love Boat* on TV. She kept the sound low so that Mr. Stamp would not know what she was watching, and held the catalog for fall semester at the community college on her lap, open to the nursing courses her mother had marked in blue highlighter. When the show ended, she closed the catalogue, tossed it onto the pile spilling from her open suitcase, and crossed to the room door leading out to the parking lot, the night. Mr. Stamp had given strict instructions that first night in Bridgeport, back in July, to always lock the door, to slide the chain into place. She did that now, standing close to the door's edge. Then she opened it a crack, pulling the chain taut and pressing her face into the tiny slice of darkness coming past the edge, but she could not hear or see anything.

Reservoir

1964

In my earliest memories there is a wooded field across from
our house and, though up at the corner there was a mall
being built, Dad could still take my brother and me for a
walk before dinner: along the path that cut through the
trees and underbrush, and over the short stone wall that
separated the private land from the city reservoir, down to
the lake where we were allowed to feed the ducks and get
our feet wet, but not to swim or fish.

My father felt just strongly enough about nature to set
up his legal practice in the suburbs. He didn't hike or fish
or hunt or watch birds, but he did come home a little early
two or three days a week to take Skyler and me by the hands
and cross the road to sit by the lake. In the summer he might
have taken off his tie and folded it neatly into the pocket of
his jacket while we pulled off our sneakers and socks and
waded in the ankle-deep mud of the shore.

In the winter we sat huddled together on a log and
watched the sun go down, red and orange reflecting off the
ice of the lake, snow drifts throwing shadows across the
colors. Skyler and I might chatter on about Christmas or ice
skating and my father might pick up a nicely colored leaf,
but mostly we sat in silence before that bit of water, staring

as if into a fire, for a few minutes, a half hour, before getting up and walking home to dinner.

1968

At a certain age, Skyler and I began crossing to the lake by ourselves. The strip malls had multiplied, and the hospital had built an annex. The plot of land directly across from our house was the only undeveloped strip left, but we might use our imaginations to make it seem like the High Sierras as we hiked with exaggerated steps, fishing poles slung over our shoulders. The wall of stones had collapsed by then, and a fence had been installed just beyond it, posted with "No Trespassing" signs. The fence was eight or ten feet tall, and would have stopped a larger person, but the ground was uneven, and Skyler and I needed a dip of only a few inches to create enough room to shimmy under. Skyler preferred to push the fishing poles ahead and slither under on his belly, while I would follow, flat on my back, the paper bag of sandwiches and candy bars gripped in my teeth.

We never fished for more than an hour, and never caught anything big enough to keep. As soon as the sun was high over the trees and the temperature began to creep up, we would tear off our clothes and run into the water, howling at the cold. We never bothered trying to cover up our activities: though park rangers patrolled the area, they generally just circled along the abandoned horse trail calling out warnings through their bullhorns. Whenever we heard the loud electronic crackle that barreled down the slope before the voice could make itself clear, we would dive into one of the coves that lined the shore, laying quietly in the muddy water with just our faces exposed. We did this out of mischievous excitement more than any real fear of getting caught, since no officer ever came down to search for us. We might reach up and pick berries from the bushes that hung over the water, alternately eating and throwing handfuls at each other. After a few minutes of relative quiet, we would resume our swim as actively as before.

We were splashing around one such afternoon, laughing at the black mud on our genitals and the purple stains on our faces, when I noticed Skyler standing still, cupping himself, staring at the shoreline. There stood the park ranger whose voice had bellowed out our last warning moments before. He held our fishing gear in one hand, our clothing under that arm: his other hand was free to beckon us ashore.

He must have said something, though I couldn't hear anything except Skyler's muttered sobs as we stood before him so he could refuse to give us back our clothes. We walked up the hill, the sand giving way to plain dirt that clung to our bare, wet feet and ankles. He sent Skyler under the fence first, then shoved the clothes under ahead of me. I remember the rocky soil on my shoulders and back, and the sharp metal ends of the fence hovering above my naked belly and scrotum. While I was still halfway through, the ranger undid a pair of wires at the metal post and pulled back a length of the fencing, a makeshift gate that he simply walked through.

He ordered us to sit on our other clothing so we wouldn't get the back seat of his car muddy. Skyler had a smear of teary mud beneath one eye, and a scrape beneath the other. There were still blackberry stains around his mouth. He chewed his lip and mumbled frightened curses. I was numb, unable to believe that this man, young, with a light-yellow mustache and round pink cheeks, was actually going to arrest us.

The station house was an old log cabin that had only recently been renovated to include electricity and phone service. It had two rooms and we stood in the first, a dark, empty, cave-like room that smelled of mildew. We were still holding our clothes, shivering slightly, listening to various officers in the other room. We could hear telephones ringing, typewriters clacking, and constant mumbling conversation, interrupted occasionally by laughter, which I was certain was aimed at us.

I whispered something to Skyler about getting dressed and running away.

"They have telephones in there," he said.

"So?"

"So, who do you think they're calling?"

As that question sank in, my father entered the room. In three long steps, he crossed to where I stood clutching my blue jeans and T-shirt and slapped me hard, flat across the face. I was so stunned I dropped the clothes, then so humiliated I threw myself down on one knee to pick them up, as he continued past me and slapped my brother, who had fair warning and softened the blow by leaning away from the hand that crashed in on him.

My father stalked past us into the room where the officers had gone silent. He threw the half-opened door back against the wall and began shouting in the deep bass voice he reserved for his most dramatic angers. He mocked the zealous trooper who had courageously arrested us, agonized over finding his sons wet and naked in a dark room. He wondered aloud if such treatment constituted police brutality, took down the arresting officer's name and badge number, the supervising sergeant's name and badge number, and was getting ready to take down all their names and badge numbers when his voice suddenly stopped and he was stalking past us again.

Skyler had begun to get dressed as soon as Dad finished slapping him, but it had taken me some time to collect the strength to get my clothes on without my arms shaking. I had only my jeans on when I followed them out to the car; my underwear was stuffed into my pocket and I had rolled my sneakers up inside my T-shirt and used the ball to wipe the mud and tears from my face.

We sat three across in the front seat, Skyler already in the middle when I reached the car.

"I'm sorry," I said as I closed the door.

"I'm sure we're all of us sorry," he said, turning the key.

1994

The stroke had been as severe as it was sudden, and there was no talk of recovery. I had come out for a visit to the intensive care unit that winter, and now I was back to see his new room. The Lakeview facility occupied the old hospital annex, giving Dad a view of the reservoir. Jim, still living nearby, had made all the arrangements, consulting me by phone, the day after he had decided.

I parked across the street from where the house had been. The whole block was gone, the woods were gone, and where the path to the lake had been there was just an alley. I spent a moment trying to read the graffiti, illegible in every language.

I was prepared for his inability to speak, but not for the way one side of his face just sagged, like a flag on a dead calm day, the muscles hanging as if by threads in folds around his cheeks. The half of his face that still worked was stolid and staring, refusing expression as if afraid to embarrass its crippled partner.

I was not expecting any sign of recognition, but I was expecting movement. This man, my father, simply stared straight ahead, past my right ear at the light blue wall behind me. I sat, my legs clinging to the vinyl of the seat despite the air conditioning, holding the useless magazine and box of chocolates on my lap.

I tried talking to him. Maria, the kids, my teaching, everything I could remember about the flight, the weather... Through it all he remained still, staring, one half of his face no longer capable of expression, the other no longer interested.

It occurred to me to tell him something I'd always wanted to. I searched for a secret memory, a forbidden feeling, a lost story. I found nothing. I was certain there were hundreds of things left unsaid between us, but there was nothing that felt so compelling that I should say it now.

So we sat in silence.

The room was indistinguishable from any other hospital room: electric bed with a nurse's call button draped over the side board, outlets for oxygen and electricity halfway up the wall. On the bedside table there was even a plastic pitcher for ice water, carefully designed to be too short to hold cut flowers.

Dad was in his own pajamas, but wore a hospital gown, haphazardly gathered around his shoulders as a robe; he had blue paper slippers on his feet. He sat in a high-backed chair that was pulled up next to his bed, his hair was combed, and he had been shaved fairly well that morning. On the shelf behind him, there was a bed pan and a yellow squeeze bottle with a long narrow nozzle at one end.

Then, without any noticeable movement, my father's gaze shifted. He was looking directly at me now, straight into my eyes. I saw not the slightest glimpse of recognition or connection in either eye, one perfectly balanced in its gaze, the other rolling slightly in a drooping socket. Despite the emptiness of the stare, there was no doubt it was no longer aimed over my shoulder, but was hard and fast at me now.

Unable to think of anything to say, I resolved to gaze back at him for as long as I could stand it, like the staring contests Skyler and I had devised as kids. I began to feel antsy right away, since there seemed to be nothing behind his eyes capable of producing a blink. I stared until my eyes began to burn and my vision began to fog, when I realized that his vision had shifted again. Whatever movement involved had been imperceptible, but the effect was unavoidable: it was over; my father was staring over my left shoulder again, the same empty expression on both halves of his face.

I had looked my father in the eye for the last time and spent the entire long moment wishing the moment would end.

I resumed talking. I told him about my return flight, my dinner plans with Skyler and Sandy, about the restrictions on visiting hours. I leaned forward to kiss him on the neck: it was bristly where the nurse had shaved indifferently but smelled as clean and soapy as on those mornings we embraced quickly before parting for work and school. I paused there for a second, my hand on his bare, bony forearm, my cheek against his neck, and remembered embracing him. I let my chin rest on his shoulder and imagined his hand coming up and grabbing the back of my head, pulling me toward him.

When I got to the car I leaned against the driver's door, staring absently down the alley I had parked in front of. I noticed that there was a pile of stones at the far end. I walked down and discovered an abandoned stretch of the stone wall that had surrounded the reservoir. The fence had a large triangular hole cut out of it and the path beyond was well worn now, littered with fast food wrappers and used condoms, but after slipping through the hole and dropping down the hill, I saw that the lake looked the same.

I took off my jacket and folded it, carefully laying it on the worn grass a few feet from the water. I lifted my feet one at a time to pull off my shoes, then placed the pair beside the folded jacket. I was ready to roll up my pants when the urge became uncontrollable and I ran into the water; my feet splashed, my knees collapsed into the mud, I knelt in the water and felt the ooze rise up over my calves. I cupped my hands and splashed my face and neck and hair and then threw my arms wide as the ripples from my splashing spread around me, blending with those thrown up by the breeze.

The Unexamined Life

"I don't see Wolitzer making the 1600."

Nelson spoke while biting a salmon roe maki in half, the bright red roe spilling onto his chin. We had become friends only recently—my divorce was finalized in March and Nelson, who was separated from Melanie, called me in late April to invite me into his food adventure. "I'm trying to treat every meal as an opportunity," he said. "Being single again gives us the chance to break out of routines; try new things."

Now we get dinner together every Thursday, mindful of our choices. Over the summer, we ate from all ten of *Time Out*'s "Best Food Trucks in New York," just two single guys sitting on park benches enjoying the food of the world. Then we spent the fall trying the best pizza parlors, two of them on Staten Island. With the weather getting colder, we were now working our way through the highest-rated sushi parlors, which were easier to get to. None on Staten Island.

"The 1600?" I asked.

We were in Uogashi, according to Yelp the fourth best sushi place in New York. Uogashi is a small storefront with a U-shaped counter that looks more like a bar than a restaurant. There is a shelf at the back of the counter crowded with bottles of soy sauce and napkin dispensers. There are two chefs, a man and a woman, dressed in identical whites, but if you watch carefully you notice that the man is her assistant, taking the orders, lining up the ingredients; it is the woman who cuts with the care and precision that makes their reputation. She speaks to no one, occasionally reaching over the shelf and laying down her artistry. Customers sit outside the U and eat facing the kitchen, sometimes standing—as Nelson liked to do—to watch the chef pare and dice and roll their dinner. Beth never wanted to try new foods and was raising Catherine, our daughter, to live on nothing but chicken nuggets. Why live like that? Get out. Explore.

"What's the 1600?" I asked again as Nelson sat back down. We had been talking about books—another area that divorce had re-awakened for me: I had way more time to read now. And go to movies, museums. I had rented a studio apartment in Bensonhurst owned by an elderly Russian man who seemed to sweep the front sidewalk more or less continuously. I had never come or gone from the apartment without seeing him sweeping, his spine bent over the broom as if that was all that held him upright, pushing invisible leaves or dust or litter toward the curb.

I waited for Nelson to answer. I knew he would take his time. He liked pauses in a conversation, liked to hesitate, as if the importance of his answers was more obvious after silence.

There were two young women across the U from us, also eating sushi, their heads close together as if they were eating from the same plate. Because of the shelf of condiments, I could not see them below their shoulders, but I looked at the clear skin, the strong eyebrows and imagined them as petite, fashionable, athletic looking. One of them—with short, dark hair—reminded me of Catherine, though Catherine was only 12 years old and had lighter, longer hair. Still, it struck me that my daughter might be like this woman someday: single, free to enjoy all the world had to offer. The two were talking, leaning in and listening to each other carefully. I could not hear what they were saying, but the music of their voices wafted across the counter, heightening the connection between us. I felt warm toward them and had a quick little fantasy that they would meet Catherine one day; that they would all like each other.

"It's a list I keep," Nelson said, then contradicted himself—"No, not literally a list. More like the idea of a list."

I had just bitten into my own salmon roe maki. The roe was salty with an overpowering fishy taste that coated my mouth and tongue instantly. I shuddered and tried to take a large sip of my sake, which was warm and slightly sour, but the little ceramic cup made it impossible to get more than a tiny sip. I gulped at my water and tried to speak.

"The idea?" My voice was muffled by speaking into the half-filled glass, making it hard to show my curiosity. "Of a list?" Nelson had a way of talking about things I had never thought of before: ideas and information that had never come up at the dinner table with Beth. I liked this thinking of new things, having new conversations and often wished Beth could somehow overhear us, know how different I was now. I looked over at the two women and found myself wishing that Catherine was there with us, instead of out on Long Island with Beth and the chicken nuggets. I wondered what Catherine thought of sushi, whether she would like Nelson, whether these two women would like her.

At night, while I sit up reading, I wonder what Catherine is reading in school, if she will call to talk to me about her homework, ask for help with something. I wonder what Catherine might think of Mr. Dubrovsky, scraping his broom along the concrete, if she would like the view from my window with that little glimpse of the Gil Hodges Bridge in the distance. That window is closed for the winter now, the heat in the apartment dry and oppressive. But I can still see that sliver of Gil Hodges and I know Mr. Dubrovsky is out there, sweeping.

"An idea about a list?" I asked.

"I mean it's not a list I have actually written down. I need the 1600 to be flexible, need to stay open-minded."

"What's it a list of?"

"How many books do you read a year?" he asked. Nelson liked to answer a question with a question.

"Books? I don't know. A lot. Is it a list of books?"

Nelson stood halfway up out of his seat and leaned over the counter to watch the chef slice a chunk of tuna into those paper-thin slivers. His large, lumpy body blocked my view of the women. You could tell he had been muscular once, but was soft and misshapen now. He leaned one arm on the counter while wiping maki from his lips with the tips of the fingers of his other hand. I did not lean forward. I had watched the food being prepared last week at Sushi Palace and it had not made dinner more enjoyable. I tried to think of something else.

That one girl's hair was a little darker than Catherine's, but still—there seemed a resemblance. She was leaning in toward her friend and they were whispering together, as if telling secrets. The friend, taller with more hair and stronger eyebrows, laughed first, then the Catherine girl joined her. It was a quiet, whispered laugh. As if humor itself were private, secretive. I watched their laughter die down; they were quietly whispering again, the friend rubbing the dark-haired girl's back.

"How many?"

"I don't know—25, 30?"

"I read about 40. I'm 42 years old. So, another 40 years of reading—82—that would be above average-life-expectancy, but no harm in a little optimism—gives me another 1600 books before I die. That's my reading life." He sat heavily.

I saw that the dark-haired girl had begun to cry quietly, and I lost focus on what Nelson was saying. I had not seen her shift from gentle laughter to gentle tears, and I wondered what she could be crying about. I watched carefully as her friend pulled her in for a hug. I wanted to make eye contact, offer some sort of comfort, but they never looked up.

"So, I have to make those choices carefully—25?" he said. You're a little younger than me, but you may only have 1200!

I made Catherine cry over homework once. Square roots. She was supposed to find the square root of 11 and she was stuck. I kept repeating "The square root of 9 is 3, the square root of 16 is 4," thinking that would help, but it didn't. I was better at homework than Beth, who—deep in her heart—didn't much care if Catherine learned the Articles of Confederation or Spanish conjugations. I can still recite the Preamble to the Constitution. I can explain the difference between igneous and sedimentary rocks or how a double-blind study works. And I can calculate the square root of 11. None of this comes up much in the day-to-day, but it's all still there if I need it. Homework was how we spent the bulk of our time together, Catherine and I, hunched over a textbook or a worksheet, pencil sharpener at the ready, filling in blanks, completing sentences, solving for x.

"That's not a lot of books." Nelson said. "Not really. We have to guard our choices very carefully."

The Catherine girl pulled out of the hug and sat back in her chair, wiping a tear from her cheek with a single finger. She smiled ruefully, shaking her head, hunching her shoulders in a small chuckle, as if she were embarrassed by her own crying.

"Just for me, Meg Wolitzer is not going to make my 1600."

Nelson and I never talk about our kids or divorce at all. We don't mention Beth or Melanie; we don't tell if we have been on dates; we don't point out pretty girls that might pass us on the street; we don't confess to loneliness or longing or regret. We certainly don't talk about young women in sushi parlors.

"I would hate to be on my death bed or maybe drifting into senility, with Parkinson's or Alzheimer's or whatever, and think to myself, I never got around to *Madame Bovary* or *Portrait of a Lady* because I spent that week reading *The Interestings.*"

That was the book I had mentioned reading. *The Interestings,* by Meg Wolitzer. I liked it —all that growing up, all that trying.

"I don't think it will take me all week." I said. "But it's good. I'm enjoying it."

The friend rubbed the Catherine's back. They were drinking sake from the same small ceramic cups we had on our side of the restaurant. Eating the same food. It was just the four of us.

"Still, was it worthy?" Nelson asked. "Of your 1600? What were you reading last week? When we were at Sushi Palace?"

"*The Human Stain.*"

"Philip Roth. Excellent choice. Very 1600-worthy."

Nelson bit his tuna roll in half, holding a cupped hand under his chin to catch any pieces that his mouth missed. I popped the entire thing in my mouth and felt fish squishing cold and raw between my teeth.

Since school started, I had been worried that Catherine was having trouble with her homework but was afraid to call me. Beth was smart in that practical way some people have. She could get things done, remember birthdays and send out Christmas cards. But she was not good at homework.

"Roth can be a problem, though." Nelson said, his mouth full of rice and tuna.

The girls looked happier now that the crying was over, as if something cathartic had happened. They sat up straighter and talked more animatedly. I sat up straighter too, watched their lips move and tried to make out what they were saying.

"I mean, how many Zuckerman novels can you put in your 1600? When can you say you're done with him?"

I watched the Catherine girl arch her back to stretch and thought of the real Catherine, last summer, at the pool. Beth sat at the edge with her feet dangling in the water, talking to Maryam Hollander. I was on a beach chair back in the shade. Beth and I already knew that we would not sleep together anymore; that part was over. But we both watched Catherine on the high board, watched her climb the ladder and stride right to the edge of the board, let it bounce. Watched her raise her arms in a wide, graceful circle, bringing them together over her head before throwing herself off. Doing a perfect jackknife, she seemed just as comfortable in the air as she had been on the board and would be in the water, which barely rippled as she slipped under. She did not come up, but swam clear across to the shallow side, underwater. As she pulled herself up out of the pool at the opposite side, I knew she would be like her mother in the world.

"It makes me glad that I read Shakespeare as a young man." Nelson said, draining his cup of sake. "How would I decide which plays made the list now? What if I missed *Midsummer*? or *Lear*?"

I shook my head, "I never did read much Shakespeare," I admitted.

"Don't punish yourself," Nelson said. "You may have missed *Henry the Fifth*, but *Coriolanus*? Would never make my 1600 now."

The women took out credit cards and began to figure the check. Suddenly, they were efficient and self-possessed. I could see that they were not girls, really, but 28 or 29, shining with the confidence of having a little experience, a lot of time still to live. The Catherine picked up the black vinyl folder from the counter as if trying to pay the whole bill herself. They laughed and haggled a bit, the friend reaching across to try to snatch the folder, the Catherine one holding it up and away from her body, out of reach.

I slid off my stool and walked around the curve of the counter toward them.

"And what about Dickens?" Nelson asked, his face puzzled as I walked past, his voice louder, as if to command attention "Sure, I'm glad I read *Bleak House*, but *Our Mutual Friend*? I mean, how many make the list?"

I had to concentrate on walking with authority and in my anxiety, I took a step too many, stood a bit too close.

"Excuse me, I don't want to interrupt your evening," I began.

The Catherine looked up at me, politely, with the kind of automatic attention you get from bank clerks or HR administrators, but the friend said, "Then don't."

"It's just that", I hesitated, standing above them where they were seated, aware of how awkwardly I was leaning over the Catherine, and aware also that I did not have an ending to that sentence. "It's just that…Well, I couldn't help noticing…I wasn't eavesdropping, I actually couldn't hear a word you said, but the shape of the—" I gestured to where Nelson sat watching carefully, his clay cup of sake halfway to his lips. "I couldn't help but—"

"I'll bet you *can* help, if you try harder," the friend said, looking straight at me.

"Marcy, don't," the Catherine said, still watching me, some mix of pity and disdain in her eyes. "I'm sorry," she said. "We were just leaving."

"It's just that—" The Catherine had turned away on her stool and I spoke to the top of her head where her hair was neatly combed, and, stepping back a bit, I kicked the adjoining stool with the heal of my shoe so that it rang out metallically. "It's just that you remind me of my daughter."

The Catherine turned back, looked at me sharply, examined my face, my posture. "How?" she said. "How do I remind you of your daughter?"

I didn't say anything at first, realizing now that her eyes were a deep brown where my Catherine's were greenish and her skin was darker, smooth and tan and more attractive than I had recognized from across the restaurant.

"It's not one thing, specifically", I said, sitting down on the stool behind me, glad to be face to face. "It's your age and the way you carry yourself. A kind of aura."

"O Jesus, an aura?" the friend, Marcy, said.

"How old is your daughter?" the Catherine asked.

"Young. Younger. It's not your age. It's hard to put a finger, it's just that seeing you made me imagine Catherine when she's … older. Grown."

"Barry, come on." Nelson called to me.

"How old is she?" the Catherine asked, her voice a little more curious, less accusatory.

"Thirteen," I said. "She's going to turn thirteen in—"

Marcy called to Nelson, "Take him back!"

"Barry!" Nelson called back. Ladies, "I'm sorry. He's incorrigible." Nelson put a seaweed roll into his mouth.

I put my hands up defensively. "I'm not," I said. "Incorrigible. Usually I'm quite…It's just that I was thinking," I gestured back at my seat, "watching you, about my daughter and who she'll become some day and I thought she might be … like you."

The Catherine smiled her tolerant smile again. "Like me? What is that like?"

"No, no, sure, I get it. I don't know you, but you work— right? You have friends, you're like, both of you, sophisticated … young, I don't know, New Yorkers."

"This is the worst pickup line I've ever heard," Marcy said.

"It's not a pickup, I swear."

Nelson stood up.

"You stay," Marcy said to him, putting up a hand as if she were training a dog. "Don't you come over here." The sushi chef leaned down and put another roll on each of our plates, Nelson's and mine. Nelson sat back down. He looked suddenly far away and alone on the other side of the counter.

"I just wonder sometimes what she'll be like, my daughter, in five years. Ten years?"

"And you came up with me?" The Catherine one was listening carefully, her responses measured, perhaps slightly amused—as if this were some sort of process she was familiar with, some part I was playing, badly.

"Maybe not exactly you, I don't know, but listen—did you do your homework?"

"My what?"

"I mean when you were a kid? A student? Were you a good student? Catherine is a good kid. A great kid. I mean that. But I don't think she's a very good student. I don't think she does her homework. At least I don't think she does it very well."

"You don't think? Shouldn't you know?"

"She lives with her mother," I said. "So sometimes... I wonder. Listen, can I ask you ... I'm sorry... but can I ask why were you crying?"

She said nothing.

"Just now. You were laughing and seemed happy and I ate a piece of sushi and when I looked up ... you were crying ... just for a minute and I wondered..."

The Catherine looked straight at me now, her eyes dark and hard, like polished wood. "No," she said. "You cannot ask me that. You don't know me and you are not going to know me. What's your name?" She looked over at Nelson who was half-standing off his stool, wanting to be over here telling us about books and films and sushi. "Barry?" She turned back to me, "Barry, I'm not your daughter. Marcy—" she gestured to the friend "—is not your daughter. We don't know you from Eve. We had dinner and now we are going to pay the check." She stood up and, looking down on me, stuffed her credit card into the vinyl folder in her other hand, thrusting the whole thing toward the assistant who leaned over the counter toward us to take it.

"I know you're not my daughter and I wasn't—I have no … motive." I stood up now, so we were eye to eye again. "You just looked like a woman my Catherine might, someday…"

"If she does her homework?" The Catherine's patience with me had taken up a mocking quality. "If she doesn't cry?"

"It's not the homework. I was just thinking you might … meet someday."

"Meet?" she said. "Now you're creeping me out." She took the papers the sushi chef held out to her and reviewed the receipt before signing furiously. She took her time, then looked back up at me. "Barry, your daughter does not want to meet me. I doubt she even wants to meet your friend there." She pointed her receipt at Nelson, who stood up.

"What does she want? What does she need to get from there—" I gestured vaguely, I hoped in the direction of Long Island—"to here," indicating the seats at the counter.

The Catherine folded her restaurant receipt, a long thin piece of paper, and slipped it into the folds of a red leather purse, which she dropped unceremoniously into a black canvas tote.

"Look, Barry, your daughter will grow up. She'll work, eat dinner with friends. She'll split the check. She'll laugh, she'll cry, she'll live in a world that has nothing to do with you. You only get to know, only ever get to see, what she wants to show you, which, if I had to guess, is not much."

"But I saw you. Laugh. And cry."

"No. You didn't," the Catherine said, her voice hard, final. "Now go. Eat your sushi. You saw nothing."

The two women turned to leave. The bells hanging on the door jingled as they opened it, letting a brace of cold air into the restaurant. I took a step toward the door to follow them.

"Sir, don't!" the sushi chef said, her voice sharp with authority. "Come," she said more calmly, pointing to my place at the counter. "Sit."

Nelson patted my stool.

When I got back to my seat there were three pieces of sushi on my little porcelain tray. The sake cup was full to the brim.

"Well, that was interesting," Nelson said. "Not really my type, but interesting."

The bells hanging from the back of the restaurant door slowly quieted, then rang again when a young couple came in. They took seats across the counter, one stool away from where the women had been. They waved hello to us, one of them saying "Konnichiwa!" with a tolerable accent. Nelson raised his cup of sake as a salute.

"We love this place," the young man said. "Best sushi in New York."

"Certainly top ten," Nelson replied.

I looked down at my little porcelain tray. The rolls of pink and white and green sat plump and inviting on the tray— each grain of rice distinct, each line in the salmon robust. I pushed the tray away from me until it clicked against the edge of Nelson's empty tray.

"Not going to eat that?" he asked. I shook my head.

We sat in silence while he ate my sushi. I looked out the window, but there was no one on the street. I pictured the sidewalk, the walk to the subway. The man behind the counter had removed his chef's whites and was sweeping the floor. I tried to remember the women, the laughter, that moment of tears, but it had faded. I thought of Catherine, my Catherine, but her face was fuzzy, as if I had not seen her in years.

Guy and Doll

Ed Bracebridge's desires grew from a love of American Musical Theater—the classics of the 40s and 50s: *Gypsy*, *South Pacific*, *Oklahoma!* He loved their purposeful naiveté, their optimism, their slick vernacular style, and, of course, their music.

So, he sat watching the parking lot of Kennedy High School fill around him. He watched parents and grandparents climb out of cars and hurry each other across the lot and around the corner, toward the double doors with the banner that announced the Drama Club's production of Frank Loesser's masterpiece, *Guys and Dolls*. He waited until the crowd had thinned to almost nothing. There was no hurry. These things never started on time.

Ed owned dozens of original cast albums, but repeated listening had rendered them lifeless. He had a few jazz records that included long-winded and self-indulgent re-imaginings of his favorite songs. The occasional full-scale Broadway revivals were exciting, but rare—like museum pieces.

He adjusted the mirror to examine the knot of his necktie—touched its straight edges and returned the mirror to its rear-view position. He climbed out of the car and, one hand pressing the tie against his belly, reached back in for his navy-blue sports jacket. It was a warm night in early May, so he could leave his overcoat behind if he buttoned the jacket's brass buttons and walked quickly along with the thinning crowd of friends and relatives, all talking with excited pride about their future stars.

He had been truly among them only once. His niece, Caroline, got to play Lola in her high school production of *Damn Yankees*, a dozen years ago; Louise had the bright idea that they should go—he *did* love the musical, and it might be fun. Louise was a highbrow opera lover and rarely joined him at the theater. She had made him see Matthew Broderick in *How to Succeed in Business Without Really Trying* alone. But for her sister's kid, she would make an exception, and Ed, she felt, should simply lower his standards.

The production had been abysmal, and Caroline had been involved in several of the low points. But sitting in that not-actually-dark theater, watching this almost-woman try to belt out "Whatever Lola Wants," he had felt something that polished professionalism had never given him. As he watched her throw her teenage body into the seduction of the obviously embarrassed boy grinning stiffly downstage, he felt Caroline's desire was as strong as Lola's. Caroline probably didn't know what she wanted, but Ed went backstage to congratulate her, certain that he had seen the moment when she realized that she wanted something.

Caroline was divorced now, trying to raise her own daughters, but Ed was still going to high school musicals.

"We're all very nervous tonight because she was *so* flat last night and then flubbed her cue on the reprise." The woman ahead of Ed was talking to a man in a tweedy jacket and a baseball cap, holding two tickets up high, as if the kids in red bow ties taking tickets might reach over and usher them in faster if the tickets were elevated. Mother of the star, Ed thought. He was disheartened by her review: if Mom thinks the singing is flat, the production had to be pretty bad. He took no encouragement from her hope for a better show tonight—he knew that high school productions rarely improved with practice. Either the kids have it or the audience suffers. He reminded himself he could leave at intermission.

He did become curious, as always, about whose parent this was. "Adelaide's Lament" was the only song that reprised, and Ed turned to see whether this was the mother of the stripper. Her anxious voice and the waving of the tickets told him nothing. That was generic parent. Her mousy brown hair and the puffing out of her lower cheeks made her appear matronly—the mother of a saint. But Ed knew perfectly well the limits of genetic expression. He had seen frosty-haired, demon soccer moms hugging awkward ingenues often enough to know that time untied enough of DNA's connections to make any parent-child embrace look like strangers wrestling.

Soon after his epiphany with Caroline—in the steamy dressing room where she allowed her least favorite uncle to kiss her on the cheek while her hair became undone in wisps under his nose—Ed realized that there were dozens of high schools within a short drive of his office. All of them had drama clubs, all of them put on musicals starring awkward teenagers pretending to be men and women. It had taken a bit of research, but Ed Bracebridge had seen the greatest hits of American Musical Theater every year since: *Anything Goes* at Long Beach High School, *A Chorus Line* at Plainedge, *The Sound of Music* in Massapequa Park.

The lobby was hot and crowded. The Senior Class had organized to sell sodas to offset the cost of the prom but had not organized to get ice. Ed sipped dank cola from a can and glanced at the crowd—solid middle class in clumps of two or three: mother, father, sibling, or grandparent. A talkative clutch of students waited by the door and a line of older boys against one wall practiced boredom. Ed noticed the woman from the line—the man in the tweed jacket standing a few feet away as if uncertain whether they were together. The man had a copy of *Rolling Stone* magazine and flipped pages absently.

Ed was aware of being alone but knew that, despite his age, he passed as one of the single fathers, that everyone would simply assume Mom had come last night. He was not actually lonely. Louise had never understood his attraction to these things. She had little enough patience for what she called "legitimate Broadway" and her taste in music ran to Maria Callas and Bach cantatas. In earlier years she would wait up for him and listen patiently to his review. His descriptions of the sets and the young actors, his anecdotes about proud grandmothers and clumsy boyfriends tended to bore her, but some nights she might sing a bit of the romantic ballad- "You'll Never Walk Alone" from *Carousel* or "I Could've Danced All Night" from *The King and I*. She had a finely fragile soprano, not really a soloist's voice but lovely just the same, and sometimes—while listening to Joan Sutherland records or after choir practice at church—she would begin absentmindedly singing as she puttered in the kitchen, breaking into quiet almost whispered Italian, barely aware of herself. Ed would hear it from the other room and stop to listen, breathing in the air that was filled with her voice, afraid to move, to open a door or rustle a newspaper, for fear that the sound of the world would stop her.

Sarah Brown, the repressed but romantic Salvation Army sergeant, was too young to appreciate the difference between sexy and beautiful. Tall and raven-haired, she leaned into every line and sang as if she was about to explode with frustrated desire. He did not blame the bored young men from the lobby for squirming in their seats as they applauded, but to Ed it was a distraction as galling as the student orchestra that could almost keep time. Sky Masterson's sophistication and Nathan Detroit's bravado blended together as both characters were played like extras on *The Sopranos*. Lieutenant

Brannigan was only four feet tall. Ed considered slipping out before intermission.

He stayed to see Adelaide. The moment the spotlight found her face, after hovering near her right shoulder for a beat, he saw she was the spitting image of her mother. Ed remembered the couple standing silently side-by-side, the rush of talking that had carried them into the lobby spent, the man clutching his magazine while Mom reached out for passing arms to grab hold of people that might listen to her repeat her stories about her daughter. In the girl on stage, Mom's puffiness had melted away to reveal a delicate chin and high, sharp cheekbones.

He shuffled through the program, designed to look like a racing form, and used the light of his watch face to find that Adelaide was being played by Tiffany Karnow. In the stiffly dutiful way she moved he could see the art projects and the piano lessons, the soccer games and the theater groups that gone into this performance and that would carry her to college where she could begin to become her mother.

She had no future as an actress. She and Nathan Detroit labored through the jokes of their first scene, and while the forced parental laughter and applause died down, Ed was searching for the exits. When she began to sing, and her voice was barely average, Ed stood, staying hunched down so he could move to the aisle without blocking the view for Tiffany's family and fans. It was not a long drive to Ed's house on Whitman Lane, and Louise might not have eaten yet. Maybe they could rent a movie. He had his fingers on the key chain in his pocket when Tiffany sat down mid-song and transformed into Adelaide.

Her chair faced the audience, and the director had set the scene so that she must occasionally turn stage left to look into her make-up mirror. But Tiffany instead turned stage right, and, her back partially to the audience, sang to the door Nathan Detroit had just exited: "In other words, just from stalling and stalling and stalling the wedding trip, a person…" and her voice cracked briefly, a sound that was undoubtedly puberty mixed with stage-fright, but which struck Ed as the maturity of real longing, of actual pain. He sat back down.

Ed had always believed Adelaide was the key character in *Guys and Dolls*. Sarah seemed to be the center of attention, but Ed could never work up sympathy for a Salvation Army brat who didn't know enough about the world to be lonely. He thought Adelaide was more genuinely in love with Nathan and had suffered the kind of loneliness only intense love can create. An actress who was any good would see this and not make a clown of her, respect her pain.

Ed had seen this in the original Broadway production with Vivian Blaine in 1957, and once in summer stock in Vermont in the mid-seventies. Now, here at Kennedy High School in the spring of 2001, that little turn of the head, that cracked note on the word "person," and this Adelaide was real for Ed.

Paradoxically, instead of disappearing, Tiffany Karnow became more real as well and Ed became absorbed in her movements—the clumsy staging and the rehearsed way her hands worked through bits of business with the psychology book and the tissues. He could feel the tension of the actress and the romantic frustration of the character; he longed to take their face in his hands and kiss their tears away.

During the long intermission, Ed could not take his eyes off the Karnows. Mr. Karnow read his magazine—the lead article featured Britney Spears—looking up only to give short responses to his wife's long questions and comments. Mrs. Karnow was a tall woman with broad shoulders, bigger and rounder than her daughter. She kept talking in bursts, as if the flow of words were not under complete control, chatting with other parents, friends and neighbors, and only turning to her husband when left alone, blurting something in a stage whisper so loud that Ed could almost make it out from across the lobby.

Ed went to the table by the gym doors and bought a rose to help support the Dance Club. He carried the single wilting flower, wrapped in yellow tissue back to his seat and dared to hope that Act II would be stronger than Act I. Though the production ran almost four hours, and the few strengths may have existed only in contrast to the many weaknesses, Ed was satisfied.

Tiffany clumsily managed to give Adelaide passion. She performed her half of the duet "Sue Me" with a fury that was beyond comic. Parents and friends laughed politely but squirmed in their seats as Adelaide catalogued the faults of the lover she needed, and Ed felt again the desperate disappointments of his life and faced the losses that lay ahead in the not-too-distant future.

He took his flower backstage after the show.

Ed pressed into the cramped backstage area already full of family and well-wishers, squealing Hot Box Girls smelling of makeup, baby oil and sweat, loud with the cheers of the cast and crew, the slap of high-fives and the shouted instructions about cast parties. Sarah Brown sat on a make-up table above a growing circle of boys. Her Salvation Army jacket was unbuttoned to reveal an athletic bra. Every few seconds she leaned down to kiss another cheek and stash a new clutch of flowers under her arm. Her free arm was a constant flurry of movement, touching boys' faces, waving to friends, or just wiggling in the air above her head.

Tiffany was wide-eyed and silent. Seated on a stool next to her beaming mother she held a cotton ball in her hand and had removed the makeup from one side of her face before she became absorbed in watching everything around her. Mother bobbed up and down, shouting above the noise into Tiffany's ear, then rising up to loudly accept congratulations from another parent, or cast member, or musician.

Mr. Karnow stood to one side, allowing an aisle to form so that a steady stream of well-wishers could push forth to praise his women. He leaned against the wall, the armpits of his jacket darkened with sweat, an unlit cigarette in his mouth, the *Rolling Stone* replaced by the play's *Daily Racing Form* program. He stood staring straight ahead, looking more Runyonesque than anything on stage that night.

Ed moved into the flow of traffic passing Tiffany's seat. He stopped in front of her, forcing the line of people behind him to stop and wait as he presented Tiffany with his wilted yellow rose.

"Miss Karnow," he said, his voice a bit too loud. She had been staring off at a circle of wildly whispering girls to her left and now turned to look at him. Her eyes were deep brown, almost black. Her skin was pale, a lone pimple beside her right nostril. Ed could feel Nicely-Nicely Johnson pressing against his back as the line tried to push him past her. The smear of eyeshadow under her lids gave her an exhausted, boozy look, but the eyes were awake and energetic as they returned his gaze.

"You are beautiful," his voiced cracked slightly as he handed her the rose. Mrs. Karnow straightened up, seeming to give him room to move closer. He held out the flower and Tiffany took it. He reached out and touched her hair, and let his hand move down to her cheek, his thumb wiping at an imaginary tear. "Thank you," he said, again too loudly.

He saw the happy smile in her eyes shift toward worry, felt Mrs. Karnow leaning back down toward him. Tiffany's cheek was soft and flush with triumph and he wanted to take her face in both his hands and gently pull it onto his shoulder, to stroke her hair as she pressed against him, to offer some comfort for the coming pain. The pressure at his back eased as he felt Nicely pull away from the strange old man touching Tiffany, felt Mr. Karnow stir himself away from the wall. Before anyone could quite realize what was happening, Ed straightened and moved past, allowing the crowd to surge and push him toward the exit. He closed his hand into a fist as though he could hold onto the warmth of her cheek.

The parking lot was almost empty. Only the most loyal family members remained backstage, and now kids were coming out, rushing to get to cast parties. Ed listened to the sprinkle of laughter, the closing of car doors, and studied the face of the old man reflected back at him in the darkened windshield: the thin graying hair, the lined cheeks. He touched his perfect tie knot again. Louise would be in bed by now, but, if he did not hit traffic on the way home, she might still be awake reading. Ed thought of Adelaide's patience and her pain. He wondered if Tiffany Karnow would think back on this night and realize she had reached at least one man in the auditorium.

He started the car and pulled out of his parking space, slowed to let a gaggle of teenagers, gamblers and strippers no longer, cross. If Louise were awake, he would tell her about the show, about the bad singing and the clever costumes and the one remarkable performance. They would speak softly, their heads together on one pillow. He would ask her to sing, and she would laugh softly, humming, maybe from *La Boheme* and he would close his eyes and pretend to hear "I'll Know," thinking of that young girl and drift off to sleep feeling the old woman breathing beside him.

Make the Man

"Closure? That's a terrible word."

"Daddy, I know this is hard, but it's been a year."

My daughter, Catherine, wants me to move on. She calls twice a week: Monday mornings and Wednesdays after work. She visits on weekends. Catherine works in HR and is very good about organizing emotions, blending the human touch with corporate efficiency. Apparently, a year after the funeral, you are expected to empty your dead wife's closet. I stand in front of that closet with the phone to my ear, sliding the door open and shut, watching Anna's colors and textures appear then disappear behind the moving plywood.

"This is just a baby step," she says.

"I can tell you've never had a baby," I say and immediately regret it. It's just that I suddenly remember her first staggering swagger across the living room carpet, her mother dancing a joyful circle around those crooked steps while I worked the video camera. The way Anna filled those dresses, her legs under that billowing skirt, her eyes matching that silky blouse, comes back to life and I stand this close to dresses and blouses and skirts and pants that look like my wife, feel like my wife, smell like my wife, but hang empty and still. It freezes me.

"Daddy, don't be mean." Her voice has the insistent patience I imagine she uses when denying someone a personal day. It's a calm, friendly voice that doesn't look back. Catherine has been using it since that first visit to the doctor.

The diagnosis came just before the holidays. A quick look at the heart, just to get a baseline, turned up a spot on the liver, another on the pancreas. Biopsy, chemo, radiation, more chemo. It was less than a year between the heart workup and the funeral. Now, a year after that, my daughter thinks I should be looking to the future.

She takes after me. I was always the practical parent, the grounded problem solver planning for tomorrow while Anna seized the day, checking the map while Anna extolled the scenery, making sure that function didn't get too overwhelmed by form. She hated words like closure. After Catherine broke up with Michael and went off to Club Med with her girlfriends, Anna declared it would do no good. "People are not doors," she'd said. "The girl's too practical. She puts all her faith in sunscreen and package deals." Anna pointed at me, locating the blame for our daughter's rational pragmatism.

But now that she's gone I can't let go of Anna's style, her beauty, her joy in the material world. Every morning after my thirty minutes on the exercise bike, I wear her black silk bathrobe to the shower and breathe her scent, still woven into the knap of the cloth. Then I hang it back in the closet where it stands out among the blues and greens, the hot pinks and the loud patterns. I put on my chinos and one of those polo shirts she made fun of and make coffee.

After Catherine hangs up, I carry my coffee to the computer and go online to admire the 401K I've built. I was an investment advisor, successful enough to have retired early. Now my portfolio has numbers even higher than we'd hoped for when Anna lay in bed next to me, whispering dreams into my ears: travel, adventure, music, dance. I recalculate my annualized rate of return and go back to that closet.

This time, I bring a box of black garbage bags from under the sink and hold them in one hand as if weighing them before I push open the sliding door and run my fingers along the shoulders of her blouses, watching the colors flip past like a moveable rainbow. I plunge my hand in as if the fabric was warm water, letting the textures play off my skin—the rough tweed of a skirt, the soft structure of a shoulder pad, the slippery silk of a nightgown. I bring out her red dress, the one with the spaghetti straps, and hold it out in front of me. I drape those thin strings over my shoulders and hug the dress to my chest, my hands slipping down to where her ass would have been. I pretend some band is still playing, we are still dancing. Then I lay the dress out on her side of the bed and run my hand along its empty length, smoothing the wrinkles. I lay down next to it and close my eyes, leaving the garbage bags on the rug.

Wednesday is market day. I try not to think about Anna's oils and spices, the smoked fish and imported cheeses. I buy bananas, sliced turkey, low fat milk, frozen dinners. Carrying the bag in from the car, I notice my neighbor, Frank Cangiano, standing on his front lawn, holding a rake and looking up into the bare branches of his sycamore tree as if searching for leaves that he hadn't already raked. He is wearing his ratty green sweater and old brown work pants, but neither shoes nor socks. I can see his red, raw feet walking in place, lifting and falling against the cold November ground.

Frank is a tough old bird who owned the hardware store on Sunrise Highway for decades. Whenever I went in there looking for duct tape or bird seed or picture hooks he was always quizzing his son, Michael. He would hold up some obscure screw or power tool and make the kid identify it, price it, describe its purpose. If Michael got anything wrong, Frank would complain that he had no one to leave the store to—which turned out to be prescient when Haley left Frank, taking Michael with her. After that, Michael only came back to the block to see Catherine. They dated senior year and all through college, travelling between Boston and that rusty mill town where Michael studied environmental science and cheese-making, coming home the same weekends. Michael would cook for us, singing while he stirred and sautéed. Later, Anna would happily point out how his spontaneity balanced Catherine's plan to climb the ladder of life one step at a time.

After graduation, Catherine got a job downtown but Michael moved to that organic farm, driving Catherine a little crazy. "Can you even make a living growing kale?" She shouted into the phone, then told him to grow up and threw the thing across the room. Closure.

Frank retired, sold the store to a chain. Now, he looked cold and lonely out there, raking imaginary leaves in bare feet. Hearing the phone ring, I rush inside, heave the groceries onto the kitchen table and grab for the receiver.

"How are you, Daddy?"

"Just coming in from ShopRite," I say. "You'd be proud of me. No fat, no salt. Nothing spicy or chewy or sweet." I sigh, noticing how empty the fridge remained.

"I just want you to eat healthy."

"Right," I say, wandering back to the living room, the front window. "So I can live forever. Hey, guess what I'm watching now? Remember Frank Cangiano? Michael's father?"

She hates it when I bring up Michael. Her mother liked to pry into boyfriends, talk about romance, but I have always reliably avoided what she thought was none of my business. She isn't about to let me pick up the slack now.

"Daddy, I know who Frank Cangiano is. Why are you watching him?"

"I'm just looking out the window," I pull the curtains back out of the way. "And he's out there raking his front lawn in his bare feet."

"Bare feet?" she asks. "How do you know?"

"I can see his feet. Beet red. And he's kind of lifting them and putting them down all the time. It looks painful." I glance down at my own loafers, a coin on each instep.

"Frank Cangiano is raking his front lawn barefoot." She says slowly, as if she is writing it down or repeating it to someone. "That's not good."

"Maybe I should go across and check on him?"

"Somebody should check on him," she says, her tone executive, forceful. "I don't think it should be you." There is a murmur behind her voice, someone else saying something. I glance back at the house behind me, empty rooms clear to the backyard.

"Why not me? Maybe I could ask about Michael? Tell him you said hello? He gave up farming, you know. He's a kindergarten teacher."

"Have you emptied that closet?"

I think of the red dress still spread out on Anna's side of the bed. "Are you changing the subject?" I ask.

"It would take me about an hour, Daddy," she says. "This weekend. We can tackle it together."

After we hang up, it starts to snow, the first of the year. Big wet flakes melting on the sidewalk, turning the dark of the grass and shrubs to something like gray. Frank is still out on his lawn, standing in the shadow of that tree, shivering when an old Prius pulls up. Michael Cangiano is texting someone as he gets out, but then puts his phone away and walks over, gently taking Frank by the arm, leaning down to say something as they walk back inside. I watch them, hearing Anna tell me, again, "You see, he's gentle. Our daughter needs someone gentle."

Late Friday night, I turn back to the closet. I have an idea that if I do it myself, before Catherine comes tomorrow, I can save a few pieces. The bathrobe, that red dress, maybe four or five of the things that give her back to me, keep her alive. I can stash them in the back of my closet. Let Catherine take everything else to Goodwill.

But how to choose? All those colors! A hundred shades of gray and black, but also blues and reds, prints and patterns, rayons and Lycra's, cottons and wool. Demure skirts for work, sweaters for around the house, dresses to go out on the town. I squeeze a bundle of things hanging there between my two hands and admire the bulk, the physicality of all that clothing. I shake my head thinking of all the times I had complained about the money she spent on fashion.

I turn away from the closet in time to see a light go on in Cangiano's driveway. I circle the bed to get to the window. Frank is outside on his lawn again. This time he is pulling the garbage cans out to the curb. Strange because it's the middle of the night but also because, though this time Frank has work boots on his feet, he's not wearing any pants.

I grab my blue cardigan and rush out across the street.

"Frank!" I call. "What are you doing?"

"Tonight's garbage night, Webster. Have you forgotten?"

"But your pants? Aren't you a little chilly?"

He looks up at me, his face anxious and angry and frightened, his dark, bushy eyebrows work up and down as he barks, "Of course I'm chilly. It's goddamn cold out. But these damn things don't work anymore." He pulls a pair of brown Carhartt working jeans up from under the lid of the garbage can.

"You're throwing out your pants?"

His eyebrows are still working like pistons and there are red splotches of goosebump on his bare legs. He wrestles with the pants' leg tangled in the mess of the garbage can, then grabs my arm too tight, his hand quivering as he squeezes.

"They're broken," he says, his voice shaking in the cold. He pulls the pants leg up out of the can with one hand, the other gripping my arm. A stream of coins slips from the pockets and tinkles onto the sidewalk, the pants rustle in the breeze.

"Broken? What do you mean, broken?"

"How do you get them on?" He pulls me toward the driveway, the narrow space between the siding of his house and his Ford Bronco, out of the wind and public view. "Do you remember?"

I look at him sharply, wondering what to do with my own fear, the angry terror in his eyes.

"Help me," he demands.

"Sure, Frank, sure." My own hands are shaking as I reach down and hook a finger through one of the belt loops, lifting them toward me. The pants are dirty from something in the trash can, ketchup it smells like. I can see that they are already zipped and buttoned.

"OK, Frank," I say, my voice calmer than I feel. "Here's the problem," and I open the button, pull down the fly.

"Who the fuck did that?" He asks.

"I don't know Frank," I say. "You got women tearing your pants off in there?"

He laughs nervously. "Yeah. That must be it."

I hold the pants out toward him, nudging his hand to let go of the one leg he still clutches in his fist, and let him lean on me—an arm around my shoulder—while he lifts first one leg then the other into the pants, turning away from me to button and zip up.

His voice returns to his usual matter-of-fact gruffness, though he still looks away from me as he says, "You want a beer, Webster?"

We had shared a beer over his kitchen table once, years ago: a tense, thirsty encounter the night of Catherine and Michael's high school prom. After the kids took their gown-tuxedo-limousine excitement with them, Haley pulled Anna into the other room leaving Frank and I to sustain a conversation on our own. He tried cars and sports; I tried taxes and mutual funds. After a long moment of silence, he leaned back to eavesdrop on the murmuring between

Anna and his soon-to-be ex-wife in the living room, then called out, in a voice meant more for them than me, "I can't say Michael will make much of a boyfriend. Your little girl will eat my boy alive." There was a sound from Haley, a half-word, and then silence. Anna appeared, leaning on the doorway to that kitchen. She was wearing tight jeans and a bright yellow sweater that showed just a little cleavage and had our house keys twirling on one finger. "We have to go, Frank," she said. "Haley's coming across for a visit. And don't worry about Catherine. I raised her to cook her men before she eats them."

After that, Haley came across pretty regularly. She sat with Anna, their two heads together, talking quietly over glasses of tea or wine. When she moved out, Michael moved with her, Catherine watching them drive away, stiff-lipped, fighting back a sob on the front lawn. Frank never said anything but over the years he managed to communicate—the look in his eye, the ice in his voice—that he held those conversations against us.

So neither of us really wants to have another beer together. "No, thanks," I say, looking up at my own bedroom window and beginning to shiver myself. "It's a little late for me. I need to get back."

I call Catherine as soon as I can get to the phone.

"Is something wrong?" There is a tone of annoyance in her voice. She likes to be the one to check on me. I hear music in the background.

"No, nothing's wrong, exactly. At least I'm all right." I hear something drop, then another voice, and I realize she is not alone. "Am I interrupting?" I ask.

"What's not exactly wrong?" she says. I imagine her rolling her eyes at whoever is in the room while she talks to her nosy father. The clock reads 11:14.

"I know it's late but listen. Do you have Michael Cang-iano's number?"

There's the sound of something shuffling and the music dims, and I imagine she has gone into another room. She speaks slowly, each word standing on its own as if she is testing its stability before moving on to the next one. "Why would I have Michael's number?" I can picture the way her face tenses up, like mine, when she tries to control her expression, hide her feelings.

"I thought, maybe, if you were still in touch?"

"Daddy, you need to mind your own business."

"No, no," I try to backtrack with my voice, put my hand up in a kind of stop sign, as if she can see my gestures. "It's just something's happening with Frank, and I thought Michael should know. Thought I would give him a call."

"What's happening?" Her voice is quick now and there is a muffled sound as if she has put her hand over the receiver and said something to someone in the room.

"It's maybe a little personal," I say. "Let me just call Michael, if you have the number."

There is another pause, then she says, "I'll text it to you now. Call him." And she hangs up.

I lay down on my side of the bed and run my hand down the length of that red dress, finger the spaghetti straps. When the text comes through, I click on the number. When Michael picks up, on the first ring, I speak too quickly, trying to remind him who I am.

"Mr. Webster," he says, his voice full of earnest good cheer. "Of course. What's up?"

"I'm sorry to call so late. I hope I'm not bothering you," I say. There is music in the background, distracting me. "But I wanted you to know." I try to tell him the story in some way that minimizes embarrassment, leaving out the no-pants part until the very end.

"Shit," Michael says. "That's worse than I thought."

"Yeah," I say. "He maybe needs help."

"I was just there," His voice is flat and deflated.

"I saw you."

"What's today?" He asks and I say "Friday," but his voice becomes muffled, and I realize he is talking to someone else, his hand over the phone. When he comes back, he says, "I can come over tomorrow. Do you think he'll be alright tonight?"

I sit up and look out the window. All the lights in the Cangiano house are on, but there is no other sign of activity. "Sure, Michael. I'll keep an eye on him," I say, not knowing what that even means.

A minute after I get off the phone, it rings again. It's Catherine.

"I just got off the phone with Michael," I say. "He's —"

"Have you cleaned out that closet yet?" she asks.

"What?" I look at the red dress, laid out on the bed as if Anna is laying there herself, tempting me. "I started."

"Tomorrow. We'll get it done, and—" she hesitates, her voice suddenly tentative. "And I have something to tell you."

"Tell me? What do you have to tell me?" I ask.

"Tomorrow," she says. And hangs up.

Frank's lights never go out. I fall asleep next to Anna's dress and dream about her, us. Dancing, close and slow, her body liquid and graceful, the one red strap slipping off those magnificent shoulders. She steps back, away from me, and lays down. I am above her, pressing my hand into her belly, like a medical exam; the dress darkens and she loses weight until the red is gone, her shoulders just tendon and bone in the little black dress she asked to be buried in. Just before she disappears, she folds her hands onto her chest and, smiling up at me, closes her eyes.

When I wake, I jump up and grab a clutch of plastic garbage bags. I slide the closet door open as wide as it will go and grab armsful of dresses and blouses, slacks and skirts, pushing them into bags until each plastic sack stands on its own, overstuffed with fabric; I tie each bag shut and start again. I want to be done before Catherine shows up to insist this brings closure, so I cross and recross from the closet to the bags, my bare feet disappearing into the carpet over and over. After half an hour, I stop and, breathing heavily, stand staring at the line of black plastic arrayed in front of her empty closet.

That red dress is still spread out on her side of the bed, and I reach down, run a hand along its empty length once again. I take off my pajamas, pick up the dress and, raising my arms above my head, slide it down, twist my shoulders through and tug the silky sheath past my belly. As the hem flutters against my thighs, I feel the dress fill up with flesh again and turn toward the mirror, looking for Anna's native grace to come alive in my own awkward pose, but see only my hairy chest and shoulders pushing out around those spaghetti straps, my belly stretching the fabric out of shape. From the window, a loud, raucous car horn gives an extended beep, followed by a voice, shouting the one word, "Pervert," loud and clear. I fall to my hands and knees, hiding behind the bed. The curtains are closed but I tremble, wondering how anyone had seen me. The roar of the engine fades; the car honks again from further away, maybe up the block. I crawl to the edge of the window and carefully pull the curtain back an inch, another inch, craning my neck to look up and down the street.

The car is gone, the coast is, apparently, clear, and then, stepping out from behind his Bronco comes Frank Cangiano carrying his electric hedge clipper, in the altogether. Naked; a bizarre pink erection jutting just below the bright orange hedge clipper he is using to trim the rhododendron next to his front door.

"Frank!" I call at the closed window. "What the hell are you doing?" But my voice simply fogs the glass. I throw Anna's bathrobe over my shoulders and clutch it closed with one hand as I run down the stairs. I have to pause and let another car go by, the driver slowing down to stare. By the time I get across to that little lawn he has butchered the rhododendron, whole branches lying on the frozen ground.

"Frank," I say, coming up behind him. He turns suddenly and I have to jump out of the way—the hedge trimmer catching the skirt of the dress, slashing into the fabric where it flowed out under the robe.

"Careful, Frank!"

"Of course, I'm careful," he says. "These aren't toys!" He waves the hedge trimmer—a flash of red cloth caught in its teeth.

"Right, of course," I say. "Real tools. They have to be taken care of. Handled with respect."

"You got that right," he says.

"But aren't you cold?"

As if my saying it had reminded him, he begins to shiver, and that look of panic comes over his face.

"Billy, tell me what's wrong?" he asks, his voice high and shaky. He reaches out with one hand and grabs my arm, his hand tight and powerful.

"Put the trimmer down, Frank," I say, letting go of the robe's lapels, circling one arm behind him, trying to turn him toward the house. "Let's go inside." I slide my arms down to his hands and pry the trimmer away. As he lets go, his finger slips from the switch and it stops running. I lay it silently on the ground beside the bright orange electric cord that slithers across the grass and around the corner of the house.

"Billy," he says, looking me full in the face. "What's happening?" He is shaking and I can't tell the cold from the fear; he grips my other arm and pulls my face close to his, spraying a little spittle on my cheek as he asks, again, "What's happening? Something's happening." He smells of filth and sweat and talcum powder.

"It's OK Frank, we're just going to go inside and get warmed up," but his knees buckle as if he can no longer stand. Putting my arms around him to try to support his weight,

I begin to cry. Tears slip down my cheeks and my shoulders heave with sobs. Frank begins crying too, and, as he lifts his arms around my neck, the robe slips off and falls to the grass. He buries his face in my shoulder, bare but for that red spaghetti strap, so that we are standing on the lawn in tearful embrace when another car skids to a stop in front of us, doors flying open as Catherine jumps out from the driver's seat and Michael from the passenger's, the two staring at their fathers and asking, together, "What's happening?"

Acknowledgments

I gratefully acknowledge the following publications, where these stories first appeared:

"Running," *Modern Shorts* (Fiction Attic, 2014); "Trump," *The Santa Fe Writer's Project*; "Even Richard Nixon" and "Returns," *Slow Trains Literary Journal*; "A Wake," *Wordrunner*; "Say A Few Words," *Storyglossia*; "The Assistant," *Summerset Review*; "Reservoir," *The Taj Mahal Journal*; "The Unexamined Life," *descant*; "Guy and Doll," *Antithesis Common*

The Price of Their Toys is the product of many years and I have benefitted from the help and support of many people along the way. Friends and neighbors including Seth Schonwald, Lou Cappelino, Bob Montera, and, of course, my family lent me corners of their lives as content. Clare Mottola and the good folks at the Mottola Theater Project have given a home to my writing and taught me more than I can thank them for. Chris Tomaino's voice helped me understand my prose in new ways. Diana Goetsch was an early supporter who pushed me toward collecting these stories. A million years ago, the great Frederic Tuten found value in my prose and encouraged me to keep writing.

Many people read one or more of these stories and helped push and pull them into shape, including Charles Foran, Frank Haberle, Diane Simmons, Jason Trask, Meredith Sue Willis, and Fatima Sheik. Nothing has been more important to my writing life than the Hunter Writers Group, especially my talented colleagues Kip Zegers and Chris Chilton. I can never thank them enough for the years of support and honesty they have bestowed on me.

More recently I have benefitted from the careful eyes and ears of folks at Cornerstone Press: Dr. Ross Tangedal for pulling the manuscript from the sea of submissions; editor Brett Hill and his team—including Grady Roesken, Paige Biever, Christiana Niedzwiecki, John Evans, Lilli J. Resop, Eleanor Belcher, and Lillian Kulbeck for the sensitive and humane editorial process; Karlie Harpold for the wonderful cover design; and Sam Bjork and Sophie McPherson for getting this book into your hands.

A writing professor once tried to convince me that one had to choose between writing and living a full life. I refused to make that choice and have been rewarded with more happiness than I thought possible thanks primarily to John James ("JJ") and Joseph, who made life more precious than art. Finally, the greatest thanks must be saved for Maria—for everything from the cover illustration of this book to the life I got to live while writing it. All the good in my life grows from her.

JOHN P. LOONAM is the author of *Music the World Makes* (2026). A teacher in New York's public schools for thirty-five years, Loonam earned an MA in Creative Writing from City College, CUNY, and a doctorate in American Literature from The Graduate Center, CUNY. He lives with his wife Maria in Brooklyn, near his sons John James and Joseph.